PH

SPECIAL MESSAGE TO READERS

THE ULVERSCROFT FOUNDATION
(registered UK charity number 264873)
was established in 1972 to provide funds for
research, diagnosis and treatment of eye diseases.
Examples of major projects funded by
the Ulverscroft Foundation are:-

- The Children's Eye Unit at Moorfields Eye Hospital, London
- The Ulverscroft Children's Eye Unit at Great Ormond Street Hospital for Sick Children
- Funding research into eye diseases and treatment at the Department of Ophthalmology, University of Leicester
- The Ulverscroft Vision Research Group, Institute of Child Health
- Twin operating theatres at the Western Ophthalmic Hospital, London
- The Chair of Ophthalmology at the Royal Australian College of Ophthalmologists

You can help further the work of the Foundation
by making a donation or leaving a legacy.
Every contribution is gratefully received. If you
would like to help support the Foundation or
require further information, please contact:

THE ULVERSCROFT FOUNDATION
The Green, Bradgate Road, Anstey
Leicester LE7 7FU, England
Tel: (0116) 236 4325
website: www.foundation.ulverscroft.com

TREACHERY IN THE WILDERNESS

Joe Bostock and his chief engineer Will Carruthers are engaged on building a railway line in the wilds of Manitoba that will open up rich wheat lands for settlers — but the Big Muskeg swamp seems likely to ruin the construction scheme. When an unseen assailant treacherously picks Joe off with a rifle, Will, although wounded himself, vows to complete the railroad and bring his friend's murderer to justice. But he is hampered and his life threatened at every turn by a crooked syndicate led by a rival contractor . . .

VICTOR ROUSSEAU

TREACHERY IN THE WILDERNESS

Complete and Unabridged

LINFORD
Leicester

First published in Great Britain

First Linford Edition
published 2019

A catalogue record for this book is available
from the British Library.

ISBN 978–1–4448–4049–0

Published by
F. A. Thorpe (Publishing)
Anstey, Leicestershire

Set by Words & Graphics Ltd.
Anstey, Leicestershire
Printed and bound in Great Britain by
T. J. International Ltd., Padstow, Cornwall

This book is printed on acid-free paper

1

A Bolt from the Blue

Eighteen below: fair weather for December in New Manitoba, where the forest, though it chilled the soil till midsummer, shut out the razor-edge of the winds that made the prairies, further south, an icy inferno.

Here the bush, which had seemed to stretch out inimitably, thinned into bedraggled patches among the upcropping rocks. A little further and it began once more; the break was like a great curving arm thrust into the heart of it, as if some giant fingers had plucked up the trees in handfuls and scooped the foundation from the frozen soil and then had been withdrawn, leaving the imprints of the great fingertips.

These fingertips were huge sinkholes, sometimes filled with water, so that they formed clear lakes; more often sodden sponges of decayed vegetable matter, oozy, treacherous, and unstable. The finger-lines were the circular ridges marking the subsidence of the mud. The thumb was Big Muskeg, which the two men who stood on the top of the humpbacked ridge could see extended beneath them.

Big Muskeg, at this point less than half a mile across, was everywhere of unsounded depth. It curved and wound, a river of ooze, now broadening into chains of lakes, now narrowing into gullies; here and there crossed by trails, but never stable, nowhere offering firm foundation for the permanent way of the Missatibi Railroad.

The Missatibi was a branch line feeding the new road that was pushing northward toward the ports-to-be on Hudson Bay. It linked with it at Clayton, whence it was being extended eastward into a virgin wilderness. Even in the days when half a dozen companies were pegging out ways for lines that were to divert the wheat north, Joe Bostock's line had been the joke of legislatures and financiers. Those other lines that were being built into Clayton passed through the wheat-lands; Joe's line ran east out of Clayton into a wilderness. Joe Bostock had secured his capital, but he had no competitors.

And slowly the Missatibi, with its small shareholders and limited means, had gone ahead. The first location parties had cleared a road to Big Muskeg. The rails had been laid halfway. But that was all, save for the partly constructed shacks and buildings for the workmen there, and the sheds for the construction material that had not yet been freighted in.

Joe, standing with legs straddling the top of the ridge, turned to Wilton Carruthers, the chief engineer of the company, with eyebrows arched and humorous inquiry on his weather-beaten old face. There was no need for speech at that moment, because the mind of each man dwelt on the identical problem.

Looking down from the crest, Wilton could see the cleared way extending to Big Muskeg's shore, and the empty construction camp. That was all; yet it was a sign and symbol of the power to come, visible to the creative imagination which materialized it into trestled creeks, with trucks and locomotives rumbling over the temporary standard-gage, to the accompaniment of the snort of steam traction-engines, the scrunch of the steam-shovel, and the rip of the grading-plow.

Wilton pictured the scene more vividly in that waste of snow because of the silence about him, drawing from it in desire the inspiration that was to solve the problem of Big Muskeg. That problem had made pessimists of men whose faith had been the Missatibi line, whose god had been Joe Bostock.

The two men had come east by dog-sleigh, accompanied by Jean Passepartout and Papillon, the one in charge of the dogs, the other carrying the transit-compass. They had camped seven miles back on the preceding evening, and had set out at daybreak to survey the swamp-lands from the ridge. For the problem which had suddenly risen up to confront them clamored for solution before construction could be carried forward, and on its solution depended the future of the Missatibi.

It was not their first clash with it, nor their second; but neither man had dreamed of its magnitude. With the physical eye, neither Joe nor Carruthers could hope to accomplish anything. Wilton was seeking inspiration, although he did not know it.

Theoretically he was endeavoring to discern some place where a foundation might be coaxed above the unstable quaking surface with trestling and crib-work, a crossing that combined the least possible deviation of route with no more than four fifths of one percent of grade and four degrees of curve.

Actually and unconsciously, he was seeking to interpret the natural convulsion which had, in time immeasurably remote, cloven the ridge of the land and set the swamp seeping into the fissure.

If he could read the meaning of that convulsion, understand the mind and mood of the great Architect, he could see, as if clairvoyantly, just where the muskeg lay thinnest on the roots of the hills, where ballast would appear the soonest above the sucking swamp. But he could read nothing. And he shook his fist at the long, sinuous, distended snake that wound into the distance, as if it were a personal enemy.

Joe Bostock wrinkled his eyes against the sunlight. 'That's what I was thinking, Wilton,' he said. 'But it's got to be done. Somebody'll build it someday if the Missatibi doesn't.'

That was the nearest speech to despair that Joe, invincible, exuberant optimist that he was, had ever made. The situation was worse than either man had imagined. Wilton felt the responsibility, for he had looked over the ground before without investigating the optimistic report of the surveyor, that there was bedrock a few feet beneath the portage.

Weeks, months of resurvey must ensue, with work halted, and the Missatibi's precarious capital diminishing to vanishing point, while the story of the great blunder percolated through the lobbies of the provincial legislature, filled with bland, jeering, ill-conditioned men to whom one day's tramp such as their laborers performed would mean apoplexy.

Their faces haunted Wilton. He remembered half a dozen whom he had approached when the Missatibi scheme was first bruited abroad. There was, in particular, Tom Bowyer, of the New Northern line, his many interests entrenched behind the bulwarks of political influence. Joe Bostock had suggested an amalgamation in the belief that Tom Bowyer could wreck the bill in the legislature. But Tom had laughed in Joe's face, and had not even opposed the measure.

'Go ahead with your muskrat line, Joe!' he had said. 'I won't hinder you.'

The soubriquet had stuck. The Missatibi was the 'muskrat line' to its enemies thereafter. And muskrat-skins seemed about all the tribute of its holdings on either side of its route. But this contempt had neither shaken Joe's faith nor weakened Wilton's courage.

The surveyors who made the preliminary reconnaissance had shirked their work and lied. Wilton suspected that most of them had been in Bowyer's pay. Bowyer and Bostock were old rivals. They had reported Big Muskeg to be an insignificant swamp with a firm underbed about the portage. It could be crossed, of course, in the end, since nature always yielded to man. But the Missatibi must either swing a huge loop around it, through territory un-surveyed, or set to itself the task of filling those unsounded depths with thousands of tons of rock.

'Damn you!' said Wilton, shaking his fist toward the valley. 'We'll beat you yet.' But he was thinking of Tom Bowyer and his gang at the capital.

Joe Bostock came toward him. 'I guess it ain't so hard, Wilton,' he began. 'I've been thinking — '

'We've made a bad blunder, Tom,' Wilton interrupted impetuously. 'Crooked work, without doubt — though I can't imagine why Bowyer's gang should take the trouble to hurt us unless, of course, they guess — '

Joe Bostock shook his head. 'No, they haven't guessed that, Wilton,' he answered. 'I'm sure there ain't nobody except me and you and Kitty knows. It's just bad luck, Wilton — '

Joe could never sense treachery nor bring himself to believe in its possibility; and if that weakness had kept him, in the main, a poor man, it had bound his friends to him with unbreakable bonds.

'At the best it's gross negligence,' said Wilton. 'Those surveyors scamped their work. I accepted their reports. I couldn't go out with the transit and aneroid and follow them all up to check their results. But I might have sounded Big Muskeg. I didn't.' His voice choked. 'Joe, if you have any sense, you'll fire me first,' he said.

Joe Bostock laid his hands on the other's shoulder, and the humorous smile came on his face. 'Well, I guess not, Wilton,' he said. 'You ain't to blame. You've done all that mortal man could do. The Missatibi couldn't have been built at all without you. Fire you? Why, Kitty'd have my life if I dared suggest such a thing.'

Wilton frowned involuntarily at the reference to the pretty young wife whom Joe Bostock had married in Winnipeg the year before. Joe's first marriage had been unhappy; it had been long ago, and Wilton knew there had been a separation, though Joe was always reticent about that.

Kitty was five and thirty years younger

than Joe, and she had intervened into a fast friendship of more than a decade between Joe and Wilton. It made a difference, as it always does, though Joe had sworn it should not, and Kitty thought the world of Wilton.

Wilton could never understand his secret feeling about Kitty. She was devoted to Joe. Perhaps that was what lay beneath his latent antagonism toward her. He was jealous of her. He was jealous of a woman's love for Joe.

'I guess not!' said Joe Bostock again, pressing his hand hard down on Wilton's shoulder.

And, at that instant, Wilton heard the crack of a rifle, and felt a violent blow on the upper part of the left arm, which knocked him to the ground. As he fell, Joe Bostock pitched forward upon him.

2

The Muskeg's Snare

Twice Joe's lips quivered, as if he was trying to speak. Then the lower jaw dropped and the eyes rolled upward. A grayish pallor crept over the face.

Wilton saw that Joe's mackinaw had a tiny tear in it, over the breast. A trickle of blood seeped through the cloth. He wrenched the garment open with his right hand, pulled up the sweater, and tore the shirt apart. The heart, fluttering like a wounded bird, stopped under his hand. Joe sighed once, but he never stirred again.

The bullet had passed clean through Joe Bostock's heart from the back. And, as he tried to raise Joe's body, Wilton realized that the same bullet had broken his left arm, which hung limp from the shoulder.

He sprang to his feet, a mad wrath

giving back to him his ebbing strength. He glared about him, but it was impossible to ascertain from where the shot had come. He could not even locate the direction within a hundred degrees, for Joe had been in the act of turning. Nobody was in sight, and the woods were silent.

His bellowing call of fury that went echoing through the trees elicited no answer. He tore strips from his handkerchief, holding it between his teeth, and, with his left hand on his knee, knotted them about a stick and improvised a tourniquet. The blood was spurting down his sleeve in jets, the pain was intense, and it was impossible to take off the mackinaw and hope to replace his arms in it; but he twisted with all his force until the diminishing flow showed that he had compressed the artery. Thrusting the longer end of the stick beneath his armpit, he passed the other through the button-hole of the garment, and, stooping, managed to get Joe's body upon his shoulder and to hold it with his right arm.

Carrying his lifeless burden thus, he

began to descend to the level of the land, the head behind him, the arms and legs dangling limply in front of him. The throbbing in his shoulder was like the touch of red-hot wires, and pain and nausea weakened him as much as the loss of blood. But he made the level, and stopped there a moment in indecision.

His impulse was to carry Joe's body back to the camp, but he knew that it would be impossible to make that distance. Yet to leave it would mean the certainty of mutilation by bears or timberwolves unless he could build a cairn of stones. And of that he was equally incapable. He set Joe's body down, and, in the first full realization of his loss and his predicament, he shouted curses to the sky.

That murder had been intended he did not believe; no doubt the shot had been a bullet fired at some nearer mark, perhaps a hare, and by one of their party. He suspected that the transit-bearer, following them up, had fired the shot, and, seeing the fatality, had fled.

But the thought that this might be the

explanation was only a fleeting one. Joe was dead, and his body must be cared for, just as if he were alive — taken back to the camp and thence out of the woods. Into Wilton's mind there flashed the picture of a pretty young fair-haired woman whose hand had rested on his shoulder at their last parting, just as Joe's had done.

'You'll take good care of Joe, Wilton,' Kitty had pleaded anxiously. 'He thinks he can endure anything, but he's not so young as he was. I'm always anxious about him when he's away on those long journeys.'

'I'll take good care of Joe and bring him back to you safe and sound. Don't worry about that, Kitty,' Wilton had answered.

And now he must face her with his explanations — and what remained of Joe. He thought quickly, and decided that there was no possibility of leaving Joe's body there. Yet it seemed to him that he could not hope to reach the camp. And now another idea came to him.

It was seven miles back to the camp,

but only five to the portage over the frozen swamp. Upon the other side of the portage was a trail that came out of the prairie southward and wound into the unknown north. Along this Indians brought their winter catches to the trading store of McDonald, the factor of the Hudson's Bay Company.

Traveling was hard along the shore of the great muskeg, but it would mean two miles less, and it was just possible to make the store. McDonald was a queer, taciturn, sometimes venomous old man, and had evinced a strong dislike of Wilton on the occasion of their last meeting. Yet McDonald would shelter him and receive Joe's body. And then there was Molly, his daughter.

Wilton, having made his choice, acted on it at once. With a great effort he raised Joe's stiffening form upon his shoulder again; and doggedly he began his awful journey, his right arm grasping the dead man, his helpless left hugging the tourniquet-stick against his side.

He stumbled over the rough ground until he reached the cleared road through the trees. Here the going was easier; but the burden numbed his right hand and shoulder, the throbbing pain in his left seemed to beat time to his footsteps, and the ache of the cramping muscles increased the agony of his wound and began to spread down his body.

Once his snow-shoe strap broke, and he was forced to set Joe's body down, pull off his mitts, and tie it. This time it was almost impossible to take up his burden, and when he stood up the scene began to whirl before his eyes. He cared no longer to continue the struggle, but consciousness, diminished to a tiny point within his brain, kept crying out about Joe, and he seemed to visualize Kitty, a tiny distant figure, and her reproaches.

He started again. A wind sprang up, driving gusts of whirling snow into his eyes. A deadly lethargy was creeping over him, and presently, turning his head to shield his eyes from the beating blasts, he saw a trickle of crimson on the road behind him.

The tourniquet had loosened. He was bleeding his life away. The blood was gushing down his fingers. Once more Wilton set Joe's body down, and succeeded in tightening the compress. And this time it was only after an almost superhuman struggle that he could get Joe over his shoulder. He knew that if he was forced to set the body down again, he could never lift it.

With knees bent, tripping over the roots of the trees, and reeling through a swimming world, he staggered on and on and on. And neither his anger nor the thought of Kitty could have kept his resolution through that nightmare of pain. It was all Joe now, the memory of Joe, his love for him, and his resolve that his friend's remains should not be torn by the timberwolves.

Joe had befriended him years before, when he had drifted, penniless, into Winnipeg. Joe's faith had been his own, and the secret of the Missatibi theirs.

So the miles reeled off behind him, while the wind increased and the snow fell thicker along the way. At last the trees opened, and the bleak shore of Big Muskeg lay before him, a desert of ice and snow, with the bluffs opposite, and beyond them the trees once more.

At once the fierce swirl of the gale caught him, whistling like sirens, boring into his face like white-hot probes. The ice that fringed his lashes blinded him, and pulled them from the lids when he tried to open his eyes. He reeled on, clutching Joe's body, and heard his own voice go from him in shouts of despair. They rolled across the snow, and the echoes came in faint, mimicking answer from the distant cliffs.

Wilton retained sufficient consciousness of his surroundings to make his way along the shore toward the portage. He might have shortened his route to McDonald's store a little by risking a direct crossing; but the surface of a muskeg is always dangerous, even in midwinter, when the apparently solid ice conceals sink-holes of slush, which, mixed with peat and ooze, does not congeal firmly, and entraps the unwary traveler, a quick-mud from which escape is next to impossible.

The portage was firm ice, although it offered no foundation for a railroad bed.

It ran between two openings in the low bluffs, and the store was visible from the further shore.

The edge of the muskeg was a litter of rocks and roots of fallen timber, hidden under snowdrifts, through which Wilton plunged waist-deep. The icy blasts pierced through his fur hood and mackinaw as if they had been cotton. His feet seemed like foreign bodies attached to his legs, up which he could feel the numbness creeping by inches toward his body. And when at last he reached the portage, he looked out with incredulity toward the opposite shore, seeing only a flickering line of shadows through the slit between his frozen eyelids.

Resolutely clasping the frozen form with his right arm, he stepped out upon the surface. The wind, which blew through the gap with hurricane violence at almost all times, had swept the ice as a broom might sweep a rink, in enormous circles, glassy and firm, with whirling snow piles round them. Wilton could progress only by inches, fighting the full blast of the gale, and seeing the line of his

19

route only in fractions of seconds.

He stumbled in the drifts, which seemed to cling to him like spirits of the snow and thrust him backward; and he held out his right arm obliquely upward to balance the stiffened body which, no longer limp across his shoulder, bore its full weight upon the trapezius, as if it were the trunk of a tree.

Yet, with his dimmed vision, Wilton saw the bluffs in front of him, and the opposite shore nearing. And he fought furiously against the creeping numbness, knowing that each second counted for victory. It was perhaps a hundred feet further. He opened his eyes an instant. Eighty now — seventy, perhaps; one last effort to cross the portage.

Fifty feet! With all of will and consciousness that remained, Wilton set his face resolutely toward his landing place, and strode on into the bank of snow piled up by the wind beneath the shelter of the bluffs. His feet sank through the crackling surface, he struggled shoulder-deep to win the last lap of the way. And of a sudden the ice broke under him, and, twenty-five feet from the shore, the snare of Big Muskeg held him.

Instinctively he sought to gather purchase upon the sides of the sink-hole into which he had fallen.

The tourniquet-stick dragged through the yielding snow, the elbow of the arm that held Joe's body rested upon the ice. One instant he buoyed himself by this means over the peaty slush that sucked at him beneath. Then, with a last cry that sounded above the roaring of the gale, he yielded. And, clutching Joe's body to his own, Wilton went down.

3

The Imprint in the Snow

McDonald, the factor, lay on his bed in an upstairs room of the house whose lower story was the trading store, and looked out through the window over the swamp beneath. It was two weeks since Molly had found him lying with closed eyes on the floor, with the flushed face and heavy breathing of apoplexy.

For two and twenty years McDonald had lived there, serving the company. Little had changed during that time. The Indians still brought peltries for barter — fewer, perhaps, than in the beginning — and one no longer piled beaver-skins about the stock of an upright musket as the price of it. Otherwise everything was as it had been in the beginning of the factor's service. The chief change had been in himself, and, since this was to be measured rather by isolated happenings than the steady progress of time, McDonald could have counted on the fingers of one hand the scale-marks of his life.

The little finger was his arrival at Toronto from Aberdeen, drawn to the New World by stories of life in the service of the famous company. The third finger was Mary.

He had met her in Toronto, soon after his arrival in Canada, and she had been born in his own town, though he had not known her there. Molly knew vaguely that he had championed her in trouble that had come upon her, for which she was not to blame. There had been a blackmailer, a brawl, a knife-thrust, a blow struck wildly with some implement; a dead man, a white-faced girl clinging to him, and then the silence of the starlit streets. Donald McDonald still bore the scar of a ripping wound along his right forearm.

That had been their courtship. The next day McDonald had married her, and brought her to the trading post. Six months later he was in charge of it. They had been happy during the years that passed before he laid her under the tamaracks, and after that Donald McDonald had lost all wish to return to Aberdeen or to pursue adventure further.

For the company holds its men. Their lives settle into the well-worn rut trodden by generations of their predecessors. They grow contented. As he became older, McDonald grew to hate the more the civilization that he had left behind him.

Mary had been the third finger on the hand of McDonald's destiny, and her death was the middle one. The first was Molly, and it was about her that his thoughts clustered eternally.

Two seasons at the mission school at Moose Lake, a winter in Winnipeg — these comprised the girl's experience of the outside world. She helped her father in the store, and was a capable judge of mink and muskrat. She could bring down a moose at a thousand yards, and guide a canoe down Horseshoe Rapids.

She had gone to the Indian camp, five miles away, with medicine for a sick papoose, at daybreak, leaving her father in the care of Jules Halfhead, the Muskegon, a deaf-mute who worked for the factor during intervals of wandering in the bush, trapping. McDonald had not left his bed since his attack, and Molly's fears were for him as she tramped back on her snowshoes through the beginning of the storm.

She did not like to leave him, for he had become more morose since his illness, and his mind seemed affected. When at last she entered the factor's room above the store, radiating youth and health, she saw with consternation that he was lying weakly on the pillow, and breathing as heavily as on the day of his stroke.

'You're feeling no worse, Father?' she asked, sitting down beside him and taking his hand in hers.

'I'm no worse,' said the factor thickly. 'You took the letter?'

'It will leave tonight. But I wish you had let me write that you are ill. The company would bring you to Winnipeg. They can do wonders at the hospital there, and you'd soon recover the use of your limbs.'

Ever since his stroke, the factor had dragged his right leg, and his right arm hung by his side. He hardly ever left his bed, and then only to sit, wrapped in his caribou robe, staring out through the window at the portage.

'I'll no go to Winnipeg,' said McDonald. 'I'll just stay here until I'm better. I'm thinking the Dog Tooths will be bringing in their peltries next week. I'm thinking I'll no buy December skins this winter.'

'I was thinking the same. The fall was too late; they won't be purchasable till the middle of next month. But the Dog Tooths will want debt.'

'They'll get no debt,' said McDonald. 'See to it, Molly! But I suppose the squaws will get on the soft side of ye, and it takes a man to handle them. I'll have to get well,' he continued, speaking with feverish energy.

Her eyes filled with quick tears. She knew that he was gathering courage, each day that he lay there, to bid farewell to the scene of his work and the gaunt tamaracks beside the water. McDonald watched her with the grim appraisal of a man who is trying to pass an unfettered judgment upon that which he loves.

'I'll have to get well,' he muttered; and his mind, which had turned from one idea to another, running from its fears, now leaped upon them. 'What'll ye do, Molly?' he demanded roughly. 'There, my lass, I didna mean to put it to you like that. But where'll ye go if I dinna?'

'Don't let us think of that, Father.'

'Aye, but ye canna stay here. I should have spoken before.' In his distress he fell into his native speech. 'Mony a nicht I've laid awake thinking on it, before I had the stroke, in the windy wacht here. I thocht I'd brocht ye up unspotted frae the warld. And noo — '

She laid her other hand on his. 'If the worst should happen, I can take care of myself. Don't fear for me, Father,' she said.

'If ye could have the store, that'd be best. But the company wouldna have a woman factor. The company's consairvative. And the old store'll last out my days and yours, in spite of Joe Bostock's folly. That's what Mr. Bowyer called it when he was here for the moose in October. Joe Bostock'll never cross Big Muskeg. And if he could, where'd he get his freight and passengers? If ever this country's opened up, Tom Bowyer will put his own line through. He was telling me so. But there's naething here but the moose and caribou and the Indians. It's always been that way; it always will be so.' He caught her by the sleeve. 'Ye'll no see Will Carruthers again!' he shouted.

'I'm not likely to, unless he comes this way,' she answered in a constrained voice, dreading the outbreak of violence which she knew would follow.

'Aye, but he'll be here. I ken the mon and his kind. The sight of a pretty face is meat and drink to him. He'll be here, and me lying helpless abed.'

'Why, I've only seen Mr. Carruthers three times!' exclaimed the girl petulantly. 'How did you get that nonsense about him and Joe and Kitty into your head, Father?'

'I tell you I ken the mon. Mr. Bowyer was telling me about him. His name's a byword among decent folks.'

'Well, Mr. Bowyer's own reputation isn't the best,' she retorted, nettled that she was forced to champion Wilton. 'You know Mr. Carruthers has an interest in Joe Bostock's line. Of course, Tom Bowyer would try to set you against them!'

The factor's face grew purple with rage; he choked for utterance. 'I ken the whole scheme weel!' he shouted. 'When you went to Winnipeg you got in thick with Kitty Bostock, and never a mail comes in but there's a letter from her. She and Joe are going to get you there, to leave me here alone. Aye, I read that letter the woman wrote you, telling you that your life was wasted here. I ken what the warld is; I learned it in one night in Toronto, years ago. And, mark me, I'd rather see ye lying dead at my feet than the plaything of a man like Will Carruthers!'

That had been the burden of his reproaches ever since Tom Bowyer's visit the autumn before. The old factor, brooding for years upon his act of homicide, had, in the loneliness of the trading post, built up an imaginary world, peopled with devils for men. And Molly's future in that world had become the coping-stone of this conception.

Bowyer had poisoned his mind against Wilton — Molly was sure of that. And Bowyer could play on McDonald's fears as a harpist evokes music. For some reason he had chosen to enlist the old factor in his schemes against Joe's line.

She suspected that Bowyer had some hold over her father. She knew that, years before, he had secured him his position with the company. As it happened, the company needed men for training — Scots; for the service has become a tradition in northern Britain since the days of McKenzie. And the company does not pick its employees out of the highways and byways.

Molly had known Tom Bowyer since childhood, although his visits to the trading post had occurred not oftener than once in two or three years. He was interested in timber and development, and other broad abstractions that lent themselves to political work and financing. But after the beginning of the railroad boom he had been to the post two or three times each year.

She had heard much to his discredit in Winnipeg, and had verified it when he spent a day or two at the portage in October. Bowyer saw bigger game in prospect than the moose, and, as a beginning, resolved to rid himself of a possible rival — Wilton. Molly had spoken well of him, and Bowyer was a keen reader of mind.

When the storm of her father's rage had passed, the girl went down and stood miserably in the doorway. His insane outbursts were driving her to the very course he feared. Only his illness kept her from going away. She looked out, her mind in a turmoil of doubt.

Big Muskeg was at its loneliest. The gale was driving the snow before it in clouds like spray, and the wind howled through the gap in the bluffs. As the girl stood there she fancied that she heard a cry come across the frozen swamp.

She slipped on the hooded coat which she had left in the store, and went slowly toward the portage, listening intently. The

31

driving wind had swept a portion of the trodden road clear of the fallen snow. In this, near the edge of the muskeg, she saw the imprint of a man's snow-shoe coming from the swamp. Her eyes, trained to observation, detected instantly that there had been a loose string under the ball of the foot, which had trailed, leaving an oblique blur across the impression.

There was the one imprint, and no more. And, as she looked at it, a gust of wind drove a cloud of snow over it, obliterating it. Molly stood up. The discovery, which seemed of no importance, passed from her mind. Again she listened.

Then, with the uncomfortable feeling that she was being watched, she started and peered into the underbrush. A pair of beady eyes watched her. They were those of Jules, the deaf-mute. His furtive gaze and his seclusion indicated the approach of one of those spells of wandering that led him to leave the store and disappear without warning. For the moment Molly was startled. Then she stepped forward, and the Muskegon vanished soundlessly among the underbrush.

4

Dead Man's Aid

As the girl stood there, she thought she heard the cry once more. At once she was running down to the edge of the swamp, and, standing her ground with difficulty in the fierce gale, she peered out, sheltering her eyes with her hand.

Then, dimly out of the whirling snow, she saw a figure stumbling toward her, bearing on its shoulder something that looked like a railroad sleeper. It came out of the snowstorm, reeling from side to side, white as the snow; a moving pillar of ice. Sometimes it vanished from her sight in the circular whirl of sleet, at others reappeared, stumbling into the drifts, but ever nearing her. It was within twenty-five feet of her when it slipped, and there followed the crash of the rotten ice beneath its feet. The figure broke through the slushy layer into the muskeg below.

Thus Wilton Carruthers came to the portage for the fourth time. And on this occasion he was saved by the dead man, for whose lifeless body he had risked his own life. For, as he fell, still clutching at what he bore, the stiffened form slid out over the unbroken surface and held him head and throat above the bog.

In a moment Molly was running toward Wilton. Once his head went under, and she cried out in despair, but he reappeared, and seemed to cling automatically to his support, for his eyes were closed and he was unconscious. His face was frozen white; it was only the contraction of the frozen sinews of his fingers that gave him his hold on Joe's body.

It was then that, in her horror, Molly recognized Wilton. She crept toward the break and lay down on the ice, groping toward him with her hands. She shouted to him to hold fast, and, finding that he was already unconscious, crept cautiously nearer over the cracking surface.

Then she saw what it was that Wilton had been carrying, and she recognized

Joe. Stunned momentarily by the shock, she nerved herself to the task of rescuing the living. She still crept forward until the upper part of her body extended across the break. She placed her hands beneath Wilton's shoulders and tried to lift him.

It was a task beyond her powers. As she strained to it, suddenly the ice broke all about her, and in a moment she was floundering beside Wilton in the water.

At this place the underbed of the portage was of peat mixed with sand, covered with water rather than slime. Molly's feet touched bottom. The water was only shoulder-deep. With quick resource she managed to draw her feet up from the swamp, and to drag Wilton forward a pace or two, thus freeing him from the clutch of the muskeg. And now she felt firm sand under her. She continued to drag him toward the shore, and, as they moved, Joe's body, still clutched in the set of Wilton's stiffened fingers, slid grotesquely over the surface of the ice beyond.

And somehow, breaking the rotten ice in front of her body as she moved, the girl succeeded in getting Wilton to the shore. From that point, half dragging and half carrying him over the snow, she reached the store at last.

She pried the stiff hand from Joe's body. That was the hardest of her efforts. Some inkling of it must have reached Wilton's subconscious, for the fingers in the mitt resisted and a spasm crossed the face of the unconscious man. Molly left Joe's body upon the threshold and got Wilton into her little room behind the store. She raised him on the bed and laid him down, his head upon her pillow.

Her teeth were chattering from the deadly cold that gripped her, and her own hands were numb, but she managed to strip off Wilton's socks, his hood, mackinaw, and sweater. His face was not badly frozen, but his hands and feet were marble white.

Suddenly the girl saw the blood that discolored the sleeve of Wilton's shirt. She ripped the sleeve from the shoulder. She saw that the arm was broken, and that a bullet, entering behind, had passed obliquely out, leaving a small but not dangerous wound. The blood had long since ceased to flow, and clotted the wound in a congealed, frozen mass.

The danger from the frostbite was the more immediate. Molly took snow from the threshold and began to rub his face, his feet, and his fingers. For nearly an hour the girl persisted, never ceasing her efforts, in spite of her weariness, and the thawing, dripping clothes about her. And at last the white skin began to be suffused with an angry red.

Then she washed away the clotted blood from the arm, and nerved herself to the task that must be performed. At the Moose Lake mission she had nursed an Indian with a fractured leg, set by the superintendent, and this experience was all she had to go by. But the break was a simple one. She brought the edges of the bone together, made splints from pieces of packing case, and wound the whole tightly with cloth smeared with bear's fat. Then she heated some broth and poured it, drop by drop, down Wilton's throat.

When she could do no more, she took her clothes out of the room and changed in another, kept for travelers, separated by a thin partition of pine planks.

She had just finished when she heard her father shuffling down the stairs. It was the first time he had left his bed. The girl ran to the door in fear.

The factor had reached the store, and came toward her, his right arm limp at his side and dragging his paralyzed right leg behind him. As he moved he supported himself with his left hand, running it along the rim of the counter, which reached to the bottom of the stairs.

His eyes were suffused with red, and his face twisted with passion. It was evident that he had seen the rescue from his window above, and had known what Molly was doing.

He dragged himself past her without a word, and looked in at Wilton lying unconscious on the bed.

'I saw ye bring him in, Molly,' he mumbled thickly. 'Ye can't fool me with tricks like that. It's a trick that ye've thocht of between ye. Ye'll cast him out again, aye — ' His voice vibrated with fury. ' — ye'll cast him out into the snaw, or ye're no longer daughter of mine.'

Molly caught at her father's arm. 'You don't know what you are saying!' she cried. 'He has been shot. And Joe Bostock is dead. He's lying dead without. There's blood on his breast. There has been a dreadful accident — '

He grasped her fiercely by the wrist. 'Joe Bostock dead!' he shouted. 'Who killed him?'

'I don't know. Mr. Carruthers was carrying his body and got trapped in the muskeg. I saved him.'

'Aye, one can see that,' answered McDonald with slow malice. 'Ye've brought more trouble on me. The body shall not lie in this house, nor Will Carruthers' neither. Mark me, lass! Ye'll put him out in the snaw to keep Joe Bostock company, or ye're no daughter of mine.'

'You're mad!' flashed Molly indignantly. With a swift impulse, she ran to the door and opened it. A gust of wind blew a whirl of wind into the store. To Molly's excited brain, it seemed to assume the momentary form of a phantasmal figure as it wreathed itself about the factor. He uttered a cry and staggered back, clutching at the edge of the counter.

'Will you let a dead man lie there, out in the snow?' cried Molly fiercely, stretching out her hand toward Joe's frozen body. 'Do you think Will Carruthers shall be flung out there to freeze to death beside him? Why, it would be murder — and on your head!'

Perhaps it was the remembrance of the past that checked the factor in his fury and brought back sanity to his mind. For a moment he stared at Joe's dead face, then raised his eyes to Molly's. And then, mumbling and clutching at the counter edge, he turned and began to drag himself upstairs.

5

Bowyer Comes — and Goes

Wilton would not remain in bed longer than two days. His hands had not suffered much, but his feet were badly inflamed and swollen, and his arm would take weeks to mend. But he could not rest, and insisted that he must return, although it was clearly evident that he was in no condition to travel.

He should have spent at least ten days in bed. Molly almost cried with vexation and alarm as she found that his determination was unshakable. By the strongest persuasion, she induced him to remain over the Sunday.

As for McDonald, he sulked in his bed and said nothing.

Wilton had recovered consciousness late on the afternoon of his rescue. That same evening his own sleigh had appeared at the portage, with Jean Passepartout and

Papillon. Weak as he was, Wilton insisted on seeing them.

The two men were of mixed race, and he was convinced that one of them had fired the shot by accident, and had expected both of them to take fright and vanish with the sleigh into the wilds. He was startled by their protestations of ignorance. They swore that neither of them had left the camp until the afternoon, and persisted in their statement that they had not heard the discharge of the rifle.

Following up their employers, they had discovered blood-stains on the underbrush, according to their story. They had picked up Wilton's tracks from the lower slopes of the ridge to the edge of Big Muskeg, and had followed them across the portage to the factor's store, where they had learned for the first time what had happened.

Their story staggered Wilton. On the face of it, it seemed an impossibility, for no one else could have fired the shot. Yet, had either of the men done so, it was the least likely thing that he would have returned to brazen out a concocted tale.

Wilton was too weak to cross-question

them; he resolved, however, that the matter should be probed to the bottom, and meanwhile decided to abstain from arousing their suspicions of his doubts.

It was on the Sunday afternoon that, lying on his bed, on which Molly had insisted, he saw through the window a sleigh approaching the store. He recognized the two men who walked with the driver as Tom Bowyer and Lee Chambers, the latter a constructional engineer who had once been employed by Joe Bostock, but had left him for the New Northern. He heard the yelping of dogs as they were unharnessed, and Bowyer's vociferous shouts for Molly at the door.

He wondered what Tom Bowyer's errand was. He suspected that, learning of their journey, Bowyer had come to spy out the progress of the Missatibi.

He was in no mood to welcome either him or Chambers. In spite of Bowyer's contemptuous tolerance of the Missatibi line, which affected none of his interests, the rivalry between the man and Joe was strong among the rival staffs. And Chambers was suspected of having betrayed a good many of the Missatibi's secrets to the New Northern.

He decided to stay where he was, unless Bowyer showed signs of remaining. But suddenly an exclamation of anger from Molly brought him sharply to his feet and into the store.

Bowyer had his arm round her, and was trying to draw her toward him. Chambers, at his side, a small man with a sharp mink-like face, was sniggering at the scene. Wilton's advent was like a thunderclap to the pair.

In his flannel shirt and trousers, with his left arm slung to his neck, Wilton yet looked so menacing that Bowyer released Molly at once, and put himself into an instinctive attitude of self-defense.

He was a man of about five and forty, red-faced, with red, thinning hair, gray over the temples, and the bold, staring gaze that falsely passes for candor, which some rogues acquire in place of the furtiveness of weaker souls — such as Lee Chambers.

Bowyer stared, and suddenly he recognized his man.

'Why, it's Will Carruthers!' he exclaimed

44

with an affectation of joviality. 'How'd you hurt your arm, Will?'

Wilton hesitated. He hated a scene, and he realized that even an attempt to kiss Molly McDonald against her will was hardly the occasion for a brawl, unless the girl asked for his protection.

Molly came quickly between the two men.

'You'll — you'll perhaps realize that this isn't Winnipeg!' stuttered Wilton inaptly enough. He was quicker with his fists than with his tongue.

'By George, it isn't!' cried Bowyer in cordial agreement. 'I seem to have put my foot in it as usual. Your pardon, Miss Molly. That'll meet the bill, Will?' he continued, keeping up his pretense of jolliness.

Wilton gulped. Tom's eyes moved swiftly from his face to the girl's. Lee Chambers, an able second in troubles of this kind but a very poor principal, kept up his snigger, effectively diverting a part of Wilton's anger toward him.

'We're just in to have a look around,' continued Bowyer. 'Not much construction being done this weather. I suppose you might think I've come to spy out the

Missatibi land. Well, you'd be right if you did, Will. What's this story about coal deposits on your property? But perhaps that's what the lawyers call a leading question, eh?'

All the while that he joked, he fixed Wilton with his staring gaze. And Wilton found himself wondering how much Tom Bowyer knew. That question about coal deposits might just possibly be meant seriously; probably it was to cover a hint that Bowyer was on the track of a discovery. And, again, it might be a mere bluff, calculated to confuse by its suddenness.

The man was as sly as a fox, for all his effrontery, and that was his strength. He gave the impression of being one kind of rogue, whereas he was quite another, as many had discovered to their cost. There were few more resourceful and cold-blooded men, even in the Prairie City.

'I heard you and Joe had come up,' continued Bowyer. 'So I dropped in to have a chat with him, though it's taken me fifteen miles off my road. Planned to ask him to sell out his valuable holdings, maybe.'

Molly, who was standing behind Bowyer, looked earnestly at Wilton. He dared not signal to her, but he caught the answering message in her eyes, as if telepathically conveyed. 'I won't tell him,' she meant to say. Wilton's heart went out in intense gratitude. It would have been unbearable to have had to tell Bowyer that Joe was lying behind that thin partition of pine. It would have been blasphemy to have let Bowyer's gloating eyes fix themselves upon poor Joe's steel-stiff body.

Yet Wilton caught a furtive glance from Chambers, behind Bowyer, as if the engineer had read something of what Molly had conveyed to him.

'You've had a long drive for nothing, then,' said Wilton curtly. 'Mr. Bostock isn't here.'

Bowyer smiled back, as if taking up a challenge. 'I'll say good morning to the factor, anyway.'

'No, you won't,' answered Wilton. 'Mr. McDonald is too ill to be seen.'

'What's that you say?' demanded Bowyer.

'My father has had a stroke,' said Molly, taking Wilton's cue.

Bowyer stared at her, and, as she spoke, they heard the factor's voice above, raised in irritable inquiry.

'Mr. McDonald's mind is affected,' said Wilton. 'He cannot see you. I am sorry, Mr. Bowyer.'

'Well, you certainly seem to be in possession here,' sneered Bowyer, a little uncertainly, and looking as if he meditated forcing Wilton aside and advancing up the stairs. Unreasoning instinct told Wilton that at no price should Bowyer learn of Joe's death before Kitty did.

'I am speaking for Miss McDonald,' Wilton retorted.

Bowyer grinned viciously. 'Well, Lee, I guess we'd better have the dogs harnessed,' he said.

Lee Chambers went out. Wilton wondered whether the two suspected Joe's presence in the building. A moment later Bowyer turned to him.

'You're next to Joe Bostock, Will,' he said in his smooth voice. 'So, as Joe isn't here, apparently, I'd like to have a word or two with you. You'll pass it on to him, eh?'

Without waiting for Wilton's reply, he walked toward his room at the back of the store. 'I want the Missatibi, Carruthers,' he began, entering, and turning round and facing Wilton. 'I guess I made a mistake in letting that bill through the legislature. I'm looking ahead. Someday — not in our time, maybe, but someday — these branch lines will have a value. I always meant to have it. It hurts my reputation, to have this dinky concern of Joe's hanging on to mine. But I guessed Joe couldn't raise the money, and that I'd get it cheap someday. Well, I was right. You can't cross Big Muskeg, and you haven't the money to loop it. Tell Joe I'm open to terms. And say I'm going to have them. Tell him he won't live forever — heaps of men forget that — and ask him who in thunder will go ahead on the Missatibi when Joe Bostock's gone!'

He could not have flicked Wilton on the raw more surely if he had known Joe was dead. The reference was like a new stab in his wound. And Wilton had the momentary impression that Bowyer did know of Joe's death, and was playing with him.

49

'*You be damned!*' he shouted, unleashing his suppressed anger. 'That's *my* message to you, and that's Joe Bostock's. You'll never get your fingers in the Missatibi. *No!* That's all — *just that — no!*'

An ugly sneer flitted across Bowyer's face. Although it was too subtle a thought to have occurred to Wilton, a shrewder man might have guessed that Bowyer had himself been under considerable tension that afternoon. And Bowyer's temper was his single weakness.

He could have controlled this side of his nature, but he had cultivated it. As railroad contractor, as politician, he had found a reputation for rage useful. Men had quailed before Bowyer in anger. The habit had become his master.

'Seems to me you're speaking for a good many people today, Carruthers!' he shouted angrily, shaking his fist in Wilton's face. 'First it was for Miss McDonald, and now it's for Joe Bostock. Though, maybe, you have got the right to speak for both of them, judging from appearances.' And he added a foul insult, half viciously, half jocosely.

He got no further, for Wilton's right fist shot out and landed fairly on Bowyer's mouth. Wilton put all the strength he could muster into the blow. Tom Bowyer, taken by surprise, stumbled and fell. For a moment he sat upon the floor, looking up at Wilton in stupefaction. Then he leaped to his feet and ran at him, his fists whirling. But before he could strike him Molly came running in, followed by Lee Chambers. She sprang between them.

'You coward!' she cried. 'Are you going to strike Mr. Carruthers in that condition? You coward, Tom Bowyer!'

'*He* struck *me*,' yelled Bowyer in fury. '*He*'s the coward, not I. Wait till he gets well! Just wait! I'll fix you, Carruthers!'

He glared about him in an evil rage, and then, without a word, pushed past Molly and strode from the store, with Chambers at his heels. A few minutes later the sleigh was whirling back along the southward road toward Cold Junction, the nearest point of the New Northern.

6

The Secret

Wilton groaned with pain in his broken arm, caused by the twist of his body as he delivered the blow. For an instant the room swam about him. Then the scene cleared, and Molly was holding him.

Her eyes, fixed on his, were filled with pity, and a maternal yearning over him that touched him unspeakably. Her face was very near his own. Wilton realized of a sudden what he had known in a dim way even before his fourth arrival at the portage — that Molly McDonald was the one girl in the world for him.

He drew her to him and bent his lips to hers. Then, because he was not very well versed in many things of the world, in spite of his thirty years, he looked as if he had committed an unpardonable insult. But Molly opened her shut lids, and the eyes that smiled into Wilton's did not show signs of any anger, nor even of surprise.

'This isn't Winnipeg, Will,' she said with a little happy catch in her voice.

The marvel of their love transfigured them in each other's sight. They were hardly aware of Bowyer's departure. It was not until Molly realized that there was the supper to prepare that she became practical once more.

'Must you go tomorrow?' she asked wistfully. 'A message could be sent to Kitty — '

'It's more than that, Molly,' said Wilton. 'It's the line itself — Joe's work — that is at stake, and I've got to be at the shareholders' meeting on Monday morning. 'You see,' he went on to explain, 'we laid out our route to cross Big Muskeg at this point, and miles have been completed. But our surveyors were either too optimistic or had been bought by Bowyer. We found, when it was too late to change our plans, that Big Muskeg was a harder proposition than anyone had suspected. There's forty feet and more of quick-mud where we believed bedrock to exist a few feet down. The records lied. And you can't lay a permanent way upon mud.

'We found it necessary to stop work on the line until we knew whether it would be possible to proceed. Joe and I came up to make a final examination for our report to the shareholders on Wednesday. We know Big Muskeg can be crossed. The point is whether we have money enough for the necessary work, and perhaps months of extra labor. The alternative is to change our route and swing a big loop around it.

'The shareholders are frightened, and Phayre, of the Bank of New North Manitoba, who is an influential one, and represents Bowyer, has had the tip from him to make trouble. Bowyer didn't want the line till the transcontinental route was shifted northward. Now he does, partly because we shall ultimately link up with it and become a valuable property. And I think he suspects that there's something in our territory worth the developing.

'The plan is to refer the situation to a commission of engineers, who, of course, would be largely in Bowyer's pay, and would report that the present route is not feasible. That would mean increasing our capital, and the issue of new stock would give Bowyer and Phayre the controlling interest. As things stand, Joe controls the company, although he hasn't actually a majority of the shares.'

Molly noticed that Wilton unconsciously spoke of Joe as if he were still alive.

'That's how it is,' said Wilton. 'Joe would take most chances, but he wouldn't gamble with the fortunes of those who trusted him, even to fight Bowyer. He wanted to have reasonable hopes that the line could be pushed through. He gave me his power of attorney to vote for him, in case of accident. And I have it here. That's why I must be at the meeting, Molly. Otherwise that motion for an engineers' commission goes through. And Bowyer told me that he means to have the line.'

'Tom Bowyer is a bad enemy,' said Molly.

'He was always that, but at least he's come out into the open now. But Kitty'll fight him. Joe made no mistake when he took her for a partner.'

'She was as true as steel to Joe,' said Molly. 'Kitty and Joe were very good to me when I was in Winnipeg last winter. You know, I went to see Joe to ask about the possibility of getting office work — just in case I had to. And Joe wanted to do everything for me — train me, and help me with all the means in his power. That's how I met Kitty. But what do you think Mr. Bowyer meant by his suggestion about coal on your lands?'

'There is no coal,' said Wilton. 'Molly, dear, I'll tell you what our secret is. I was pledged to Joe — but the secret's mine now, and I can tell you. It isn't coal — it's *clay.'*

'Clay, Wilton?'

'Clay. It's more valuable than coal or gold. It's clay land that the wheat grows on, or rather in the rich topsoil of loam, with the clay subsoil to seal and preserve the rainfall, yet easily drained with a little labor.

'I discovered it when I was prospecting up this way four years ago. It's probably an extension of the New Ontario clay belt, and, if so, it runs for hundreds of miles through this part of Northern Manitoba. It means that the wheat area of Canada will be increased by thousands of square miles. It means the clearing of the bush, settlers, homes, fertile lands, and huge harvests where the forests and the Indians have been since the beginning of time. It means homes and prosperity for thousands who are now struggling for a bare living in our cities.

'That appealed to Joe. He was a man, if ever there was one. He saw the money in it, and the value of the line, but he saw further than that. He was looking ahead, years after he was gone. He wanted to do good in his own way. He'd had a hard time when he was a young man. And because people believed in Joe, though he dared not tell them his secret, they lent him the capital, and took up his shares. That was Joe's dream — and it's mine, Molly.'

She listened breathlessly as he revealed his dream to her, and yet, perhaps, womanlike, she was happy rather in the revelation of himself than in the altruism of the dead man.

'That's what the Missatibi meant to Joe,' said Wilton. 'That's why we mean to fight to keep it out of Bowyer's hands. Molly, dear, when I realized that Joe was dead everything seemed ended for the line. I couldn't see how we were going to carry on without him. It's only now — now that I have found something as well as lost everything — that I can begin to pick up my courage.'

She laughed and put her face down on his shoulder.

'No other man could have got money for such a road without divulging his purpose,' continued Wilton. 'No other man could have begun a line out into the bush, with the mere promise of someday completing it southward to join another line that didn't exist.

'Well, when Joe's death came home to me I thought things over in there, and it seemed to me that the only thing possible for me would be to go before the shareholders and tell them frankly what lay behind the enterprise — I mean the clay lands and their development.

'But, Molly, I've changed my mind. I won't tell them. I'll keep control for Kitty. Joe and I agreed that, if we told them, we couldn't keep the line from Bowyer and his crowd. The knowledge would have brought all the predatory interests in the province down on us. They'd buy and buy, and send the shares up until the little investors, tucked away in the country places, who knew Joe, felt forced to sell their shares.

'Bowyer would wreck the line, and there'd have been an end of all Joe's dreams. I won't tell them. And I'll advise the shareholders to proceed with the route we've planned. I'll take the responsibility. Big Muskeg can be crossed. It shall be.

'And I'll do more than that, Molly. I'll get the shareholders' authorization before they know Joe's dead. If they knew that, it'd be all up with the line. Bowyer doesn't know. Nobody knows except ourselves. I don't like doing that. But I'm fighting for Kitty now, and Joe would have approved.'

He stopped and laughed at his own vehemence. 'I've told you all this, Molly,' he said, 'because you have the right to know. And just as soon as we've won I shall be in a position to ask you to be my wife, Will you, dear?'

Molly turned and put her hands on his shoulders. 'Yes, Will,' she answered. 'And I hope with all my heart that you succeed in carrying out Joe's plans. And I believe you will. And I believe you will find a way to cross Big Muskeg. I see now that I must let you go, though I can't bear to, Will. But now I must say something. You know my father — '

'Doesn't altogether approve of me as a son-in-law, to put it mildly,' answered Wilton. 'I can't make out the reason for his dislike of me. The first time I came here we struck up a friendship that looked as if it would be good for all time. Do you know what the trouble is, Molly?'

'I'm afraid Tom Bowyer has been influencing him against you. He has a strong power over Father. He helped him in some way when he first came to this country.'

'Then that's another score against our friend Bowyer,' said Wilton.

'But I was going to say — you see, my

father's mind has given way to some extent since his stroke, and — I don't know, Will, dear, but I'm almost afraid he is never going to be the same man again. It started even before his attack — this feeling against you, and his moroseness. It began when Tom Bowyer was here last autumn.'

'Your father wasn't over-pleasant to me the second time I came. The third time he was distinctly disagreeable. Both those times must have been after Bowyer's visit.'

'Yes. The second time you came was a few days after he had been here. I'm afraid Tom Bowyer slandered you to Father. And I think it was my father's brooding over things that really caused his illness. So we'll just have to be patient. And I'm going to ask you, for the present, not to say anything about this to him.'

Wilton promised, though with reluctance. He did not like the concealment. His mind, simple and direct, worked in straightforward ways. However, he had been too hard hit over Joe's death to make room for a new trouble. And he could not have refused Molly.

7

'In the King's Name!'

But he worried over the situation all night, and in the morning Molly saw with alarm that he was in a feverish condition. He should never have left his bed, and the journey seemed impossible.

'I've got to go, Molly,' was all Wilton could say.

'Then,' she said with sudden decision, 'I shall go with you.'

He tried to laugh at her, but she insisted.

'I shall go, Will,' she said. 'You can't travel alone. Your men may be faithful enough, but it is my right to go. And you'll never get to the meeting without someone to take care of you on the way. That's my condition. Promise me — or else I'll lock the store door, Will, and I've got a padlock that even you couldn't force.'

Molly seemed to be animated by a resolution as feverish as his own. Jules Halfhead had not fulfilled his intention of absenting himself, probably on account of the storm, which had made the security of the store seem preferable to life in the forests. He was faithful to the factor, and had never deserted him in need. He could take care of him during the four or five days of her absence.

'And Kitty will be glad to have me stay with her,' said Molly. 'I'll be a comfort to her in her grief. And I feel that I ought to go, if only for Kitty's sake. I know she hasn't made many friends in Clayton yet. And she is always writing to me to come.'

Wilton was forced to yield. 'But you must make sure that Jules will stay,' he said.

'He'll understand. He'll stay,' answered the girl. 'He's never run away when I was gone to Moose Lake or Winnipeg.'

Molly went up to the factor's room with the faint hope of reaching some understanding — of plumbing her father's feeling against Wilton and overcoming it.

'Mr. Carruthers is getting ready to go,'

she said. 'He is very ill. He is too weak to travel alone, but he must take Joe Bostock's body back to Clayton.'

'Oh, aye!' said the factor, sneering.

'He needs care and attention during the journey. So I am going with him.'

The factor sat up in bed, transfixing her with a look of fury. 'You, lass — you will go with Wilton Carruthers to Clayton!' he cried. 'Ye winna come hame, then! Mark me, now, I've done with you for aye!'

'Would you have him die in the snow?' cried the girl, with almost equal anger.

'Aye, I'd have him die in the snaw, like the dog that he is!' he answered. 'If he'd died with Joe Bostock, the warld could ha' spared the twa of them. Molly, lass, ye winna go!' he pleaded, with a sudden change of tone. 'Think of your good name in Clayton! I havena reared ye to have ye desert me in my old age and sickness, Molly.'

She turned quickly away to keep her tears from falling. 'Jules can take care of you for a few days, Father,' she said. 'It's not as if you were helpless. And his life is at stake.'

'And mebbe he'll die if you don't stay

with him when ye get to Clayton, eh, lass?' rasped out the factor in withering scorn.

That scorn nerved her again; to his weakness she had almost yielded. She went down and dressed herself for the journey. She helped Wilton on with his mackinaw, and put a caribou robe in the sleigh. Then, while the men were harnessing the dogs, struck by a sudden thought, she stooped and began to examine the tracks of the snowshoes about the edge of the portage. They ran confusedly in all directions, for the marks had been made by seven different pairs — those of Bowyer and Chambers and their Indian; those of Wilton and his two men; those of the deaf-mute.

Of these Wilton's were blurred and almost indistinguishable, made by his dragging feet as she pulled him up from the swamp. But, even had the vague purpose in Molly's mind been clear to her, there would have been no need to examine those. The rest were all similar in one respect — none had a broken string.

Wilton and Molly had arranged that he was to travel in the sleigh, to which a second had been attached, bearing Joe's body in a roughly made coffin constructed by the men. The dogs were harnessed, and they started.

It was a little more than fifty miles to Clayton. Traveling along the cleared road, the distance could be quickly covered easily in two days. Halfway, at the head of the narrow-gage line, was a cache, in charge of a keeper, who also guarded the supplies and material in the sheds. Here the first night was to be passed; the second evening should see them at their destination.

The dogs ran well, the weather was clear and fine, and Wilton felt well enough to walk a good deal. Their dinner was almost like a picnic. By evening the rail-head had come into sight in the distance, the empty camp, the long sheds with the miscellany of supplies, the locomotive shops, and the great ballast pits beside the line.

Here, too, began the telephone poles, extending into Clayton; but the linemen's rough work had not been proof against the weight of the snow, and the wires hung in festoons from post to post. The installation had hardly been made before work was abandoned, and there was no connection now at Clayton.

As the dogs climbed the last hill, there came yelping from the cleared way behind them. Looking back, they perceived a sled approaching. Two men walked beside it, and the dogs, sighting Wilton's, yelped in challenge, which was taken up in an outburst of answering growls.

The sled drew in toward them, and the men resolved themselves into sergeant and a constable of the mounted police. Wilton had stopped his dogs, but the newcomers did not halt, and went on, with curt greetings, toward the cache.

A little surprised at their abruptness, Wilton let the sled precede his sleigh. As the dogs were eager for their meal, he sent Papillon ahead with them, and followed more leisurely with Molly. They arrived at the cache a few minutes after the two men, to find the two policemen waiting for them, while the other men were unharnessing the dogs. Andersen, the old Swedish caretaker, was standing beside Joe's coffin with a stunned look on his face. The policemen were not of prepossessing appearance. The elder man, the sergeant, was about forty years of age. He had a fair, drooping mustache, a slight cast in one eye, and an expression of sullen insolence. His companion, a short, stocky young fellow, looked hardly less surly and evidently ill at ease.

'Evening, Mr. Carruthers,' said the sergeant brusquely. 'I'm Sergeant Peters, and this is Constable Myers. That's Joe Bostock's body you're bringing in, I guess.'

Wilton was staggered. 'Yes, it's Joe!' he said, gulping. 'How did you get the news?'

The policemen exchanged glances. Peters smiled scornfully under his long mustache. 'It's known, all right. It's our job to know them things,' he answered. 'I'm taking charge of it — to bring it in for the inquest.'

'But you are not from Clayton,' said Wilton, who, of course, knew all the members of the small force of police that was stationed there.

'We're from the Pas,' answered the sergeant shortly.

From the Pas! That explained how the sled had come along the road behind him. Bowyer must have discovered the fact of Joe's death in some manner, and had probably spread the news. Wilton surmised that Jules Halfhead had somehow managed to indicate the fact to him. But it seemed impossible that Bowyer could have reached Cold Junction, his construction camp and the head of his telephone posts, even by this time, much less have been able to obtain a detail of police from the Pas.

The constable solved his problem. 'We was on patrol,' he vouchsafed. 'And we met parties who told us about Joe Bostock having met with an accident, and that you was bringing him in.'

'That'll be all!' snapped the sergeant, looking angrily at Myers, who subsided promptly. 'I guess this young woman is Molly McDonald?' he continued.

'This lady is Miss McDonald,' said Wilton angrily, 'and you'll keep a civil tongue in your head, sergeant.'

Peters looked him up and down insolently, and for a moment or two the men faced each other in an aggressive attitude. Then the sergeant, sneering, swung on his heel. Wilton did not know what to make of his attitude, for the police were always friendly. At first it occurred to him that the sergeant might have taken him, in his bush outfit, for any laborer, but then he remembered that he had addressed him by name. In any event, it would be impossible to ask him who had informed him of Joe's death.

The constable, who was evidently under strict orders, seemed more inclined to talk, but glanced nervously at his superior. Wilton finally ascribed the man's manner to the nervousness of new hands at the business — at any rate, in that district. Andersen's room was placed at Molly's disposal, and after Wilton had seen to her comfort he went outside the shack.

The dogs were yelping and snarling over their fish from the cache. Papillon had just finished feeding them, and Wilton thought Peters had been speaking, to him. Probably the sergeant was trying to obtain information. A momentary surge of anger made him clench his fist; then he shrugged his shoulders and went into the shack where Andersen was preparing the meal. Peters and Myers had already shaken down their blankets on the floor, and Jean Passepartout had laid down Wilton's, and the caribou robe, but the Indians' were not there.

The Swede came up to Wilton, holding a pan of sizzling brown potatoes. 'I can't believe it, Mr. Carruthers,' he said. 'Only last week he passed through here with you. Gosh, he was a fine man, Joe was! How did it happen? And you're hurt yourself, sir,' he continued, glancing at Wilton's arm.

'Joe was shot at my side in the woods. The same bullet hit me. I don't know who fired the shot. But I'm *going* to know,' said Wilton grimly.

'My God, it's all up with the line yet!' muttered the old man, withdrawing to his fire.

Wilton looked at Molly, who had come out of the bedroom and was standing near him. Andersen's exclamation had gaged the whole situation. Wilton felt physically nauseated by the heat in the shack, the unpleasantness of the situation, and a recurrence of pain in his wound.

'I wish we could get on, Molly,' he muttered. 'I don't know what to make of this business; but I don't believe that Joe's death is known in Clayton yet. If these men were on patrol, of course, they could have got here the way they did, but who told them? Bowyer couldn't have been lurking out in the snow all this time. Well, it'll all come out,' he added wearily. 'But I hate to pass the night here, with those two men keeping watch over Joe, and accompanying us in with him in the morning.'

He went over to Andersen. 'Do you happen to know either of those fellows?' he asked.

'I never saw them before, sir,' said the old man. 'I guess they ain't from these parts, from the looks and the ways of 'em.'

'There's a new lot come up from Yorkton lately. Maybe they shifted these to the Pas when they sent some of the Pas men on to Clayton,' Wilton reflected. He turned to Molly. 'Anyway, we'll start bright and early,' he said. 'I suppose we'll have to have those fellows' company as far as Clayton. But I wonder — ' He paused. 'I wonder whether Joe would forgive me for leaving him in the hands of strangers for a while, if it were for Kitty?' he mused.

The two policemen came in, looking surly and uncommunicative as ever. After a hurried meal, eaten almost in silence, they swept back the tablecloth, pulled the oil lamp into their corner, and produced a deck of cards. Molly said good night to Wilton and went into the caretaker's room. As the door closed behind her Wilton saw the two men look after her. The constable whispered something to the sergeant, and both chuckled.

Wilton's blood was boiling, but he controlled himself. This was for Kitty, and his debt to Joe.

At last the policemen put the cards away, and prepared to lie down. Andersen was already snoring upon the floor. His two men, however, had not come in, and Wilton, going to the stables, found them curled up among the huskies.

'You fellows had better come into the shack,' he said, 'unless you want to freeze.'

Papillon refused. 'Them damn dogs will fight each other,' he said, 'if we don't stay here.'

'Just as you like,' said Wilton.

It was not unusual for rival teams of huskies to attack each other, but such antipathy generally developed from the first, and the dogs seemed contented enough. He went back to the shack and lay down, turning over in his mind what he was projecting, but he was utterly worn out, and fell asleep before he was aware of it.

When he opened his eyes it was already dawn. The policemen were dressed and standing outside the shack, conversing in low tones. Andersen was peeling potatoes for breakfast. Wilton heard Molly moving within the room, and his doubts fell from him. He had been upset by the surliness of the two men; he had had vague suspicions not justified in fact. He determined to put his proposal to them.

He walked over to the sergeant, who

was just re-entering the shack with his companion. 'I suppose you fellows are thinking of starting at once, after breakfast,' he suggested.

The sergeant looked him up and down. 'That's about the size of it,' he growled. 'Got any objection?'

Wilton resolutely ignored the affront. 'I've got important business in Clayton, affecting Mr. Bostock's interests,' he said. 'It is very important that his death should not be known there until midday tomorrow.'

The constable, who was leaning against the door-post, chewing the end of a twig, started slightly. Peters fixed Wilton with his crooked stare. 'Rather a nervy thing to propose, Mr. Carruthers!' he sneered.

'Maybe, but it's a business matter affecting Mr. Bostock's wife,' said Wilton, loathing himself for making the request, but nerving himself to do so by the thought of Kitty. 'If the news of his death reaches Clayton before the time I've mentioned, some people who are antagonistic to Mr. Bostock's interests will jump at the chance to turn it to account. It will mean a heavy loss to Mrs. Bostock. You've come a long way, and you could quite reasonably wait till afternoon on account of the dogs. That will bring you in before noon tomorrow. And — if you can see your way to it, you two won't be the losers.'

The sergeant eyed him more insolently than ever. 'So that's the program, is it?' he answered. 'Well, keep your mind easy. The news won't be known in Clayton tonight, nor tomorrow neither. We ain't going to Clayton.'

'You're not, eh? Then where the devil are you going?' cried Wilton, nettled almost beyond endurance at the man's demeanor.

'We're taking Joe Bostock's body back to the Pas,' retorted the sergeant. 'That's what we come here for.'

'The Pas? This isn't in the Pas jurisdiction!'

'It ain't, eh? Perhaps it's in yours, then?'

'See here,' cried Wilton in exasperation, 'Clayton has its own police detachment, as you know perfectly well. Your route doesn't lie in this direction. Joe Bostock's home's there. He's going to be buried there. And his body isn't going to be dragged here and there about the country by a couple of fool policemen. I'll make things pretty warm for you if you try any game like that.'

'You will, eh?' sneered the sergeant, with a side glance at Myers. 'Got any sort of special pull in Clayton?'

'Enough to put the lid on you.'

'Well, I guess you won't be going into Clayton yet a while,' jeered Peters. 'You're coming back to the Pas with us and Joe.'

Wilton realized that Myers had come up quietly upon the other side of him. He had the bewildered feeling of being in a trap. 'What the devil do you mean by that?' he shouted.

The sergeant thrust his face forward into his own, grinning maliciously. 'It means that I arrest you for the willful murder of Joe Bostock,' he answered. 'And I warn you, in the king's name, that any statement you make will be used against you.'

8

Assault and Battery

At the same moment Wilton felt the touch of steel against his right wrist, and swung his hand free just in time to avoid the snap of the handcuff. Looking at Sergeant Peters after the instant's sideward glance, he found himself covered by the heavy regulation .45 Colt. Before he could stir, Myers had seized him from behind and made a violent effort to slip the handcuff upon his wrist.

Wilton heard Molly scream. The girl came running out of the room with her hair tumbling about her shoulders, and caught at Myer's arm. The caretaker started toward them, still holding the frying pan, in which he was cooking the potatoes, his face working with rage.

'You damn fools!' he shouted, lapsing into his vernacular in his excitement. 'You got it all wrong! Mr. Carruthers was Joe's best friend. So that was your game when you come here last night, eh? You'll get broke for this job already, both of you fellers, I tell you.'

Molly was grasping at Myers' hand as the constable still fumbled nervously with the handcuff. 'Won't you men listen to common sense?' she cried. 'Mr. Carruthers is the chief engineer of the line. All his interests are bound up with it. Why should he want to murder Joe? He was Joe's best friend. Everyone in Clayton can tell you that. Why, he risked his own life to save him! Somebody's put you on the wrong track. They're trying to make use of you to keep him out of the way while they ruin the line. And you'll pay for your mistake, that's sure!'

And, with frenzied desperation, she succeeded in pushing Myers away from Wilton, and interposed between him and the sergeant, whose revolver pointed steadily at his forehead.

Peters scowled viciously at her. 'You can tell all that at the inquest,' he snapped. 'I've got orders to bring you in, too. Get out of the way!'

At that, the superhuman tension that held Wilton's rage in bounds seemed to snap. His ears were ringing, and a spotted mist floated before his eyes. Through this he saw Peters an infinite distance away, the revolver, now hardly larger than a pencil, pointing at his head. Behind the sergeant he saw Andersen, a doll-like figure with a toy pan in his hand. He leaped at Peters, heard the weapon discharged, and was conscious of the sting of powder on his forehead and a commotion in his hair.

Peters had shot to kill, but the weapon, the least bit diverted by Molly's intervention, had been re-aimed at Wilton's forehead a little hurriedly, and he had forgotten that the strong ammunition, of which complaint had frequently been made by the police superintendents, was apt to throw the bullet high at short distances.

Wilton shot his uninjured arm forward with a vicious swing that caught the sergeant on the cheek and sent him staggering backward. But the force of the blow, communicated to Wilton's left shoulder, wrenched the wound and forced a groan of pain from his lips. Peters reeled, regained his balance, and rushed forward again, swinging the revolver aloft, butt forward, in his hand.

With his powerful build, he could have delivered a blow that would have crushed Wilton's skull. But before the blow fell, Andersen had raised his pan and brought it down edgewise upon the sergeant's head, cutting the scalp to the bone and drenching the man with the boiling grease.

With a scream of pain, Peters stumbled forward, letting the revolver fall from his hand, slipped in the grease that had begun to ooze along the floor, and fell full length on the planks, where he lay writhing in anguish, and trying to clear his eyes of the melted fat and the blood that streamed down his forehead.

Instantly Molly stooped, snatched up the weapon, which had fallen at her feet, and covered the constable, who had flung himself upon Wilton again. Myers stopped dead and threw his hands up automatically.

'Get over there!' said Molly briskly, pointing toward the wall behind the sergeant.

Myers obeyed immediately, and took

his post against the wall, the picture of confusion. Peters struggled slowly to his feet. His predicament would have been ludicrous under less serious circumstances. His face and pea-jacket were covered with a film of grease, over which the blood from his wound was trickling. The tables were turned with dramatic completeness.

'You know what this means!' spluttered the sergeant, trying to clear the fat from his eyes.

'I do, and I'll take my chance,' answered Wilton, gritting his teeth at the pain from his injured arm. The wound did not seem to have reopened, but either his blow or the grasp of the constable had displaced the broken ends of the bone, and he could feel them grating together at his slightest movement. 'Keep your hands up, both of you!' he ordered. 'Give me the revolver, Molly! Got a rope, Andersen?'

'Well, I guess I have,' grinned the Swede. He stepped to a packing-case behind the stove, and brought out a short coil of manila, which, with a kitchen knife, he sliced into four or five lengths.

'I tank I tie them to that beam,' he said, indicating one of the vertical uprights of the wooden shack.

'All right, Andersen,' said Wilton. 'Tie 'em so that they can sit down. They'll have some time to wait, and they may get tired standing.'

He took the revolver from Molly and slipped it into his pocket. Peters let loose a string of vicious oaths as Andersen proceeded to truss him up, but neither man offered any resistance. The caretaker fastened an end of rope securely round the body of each, tying him to the beam. He then secured the four ends together in a knot that looked able to defy even an expert. With other pieces he bound the policemen's wrists together, and also their legs. This done, he stepped back and looked at his work with critical satisfaction.

'I tank you get to Clayton by tomorrow night, all right, Mr. Carruthers,' he said with droll complacency, putting some more potatoes in the pan.

And, with complete nonchalance, he set the coffee on the table and filled two plates with steaming hash. 'After we've ate I'll untie you fellows' hands, if you're good boys, and give you some breakfast,' he said soothingly to the captives.

'You go to hell!' snarled Peters. 'You'll pay for this outrage, every man jack of you. And you, too,' he shouted to Molly.

'Maybe you're right,' returned the Swede, sitting down beside Molly and Wilton. 'But it's fun while it lasts, ain't it?'

Despite their elation, Molly and Wilton took only a few mouthfuls, washing down the food, which they could hardly masticate, with gulps of coffee. They were glad to get out into the air. It was a dull day, and a few flakes of snow were beginning to drift down, while the intense stillness of the air presaged a storm. Wilton made his way to the cache, unlocked it, and took out some frozen fish for the dogs, which were giving tongue vigorously inside the stable.

'Here, Papillon!' he called. 'I can't make out what's the matter with those men, lying in their blankets at this hour, with the dogs howling for their breakfast,' he said to Molly indignantly. 'They must have known I'd feed them before starting on a run like the one we've got before us. I suppose they heard the row and got scared back to bed,' he added.

But no answer came to his call, and suddenly Molly uttered a cry and pointed. On the other side of the stable were the tracks of a sleigh, obliterated at the entrance by the falling snow, which had drifted against the building.

Wilton wrenched the door open. His sleigh and the dogs were gone, together with the rifle, shotgun, and transit-compass. Their two workers had deserted during the night. They had taken the compass probably because it was in the sleigh, and the weapons by choice. The tracks ran straight across country northward, along one of the trails that had been hewn by the first location party.

They took in the situation swiftly.

'They must have guessed that those men meant to arrest you, or else they heard them talking,' said Molly.

But Wilton had hurried to the horse-stalls, separated from the dog-stable by a stout door. He breathed a deep sigh of relief. The second sleigh was there. For a moment the thought of possibilities had made his heart almost stand still.

He came back grim and resolute. 'There's something pretty deep in all this business,' he said. 'I know why the men ran away. The sergeant gave them the tip to. I saw him talking to Papillon last night. And that's the reason why they wouldn't sleep in the shack — because they meant to run. I suppose the policemen were afraid that they would make trouble, or try to help us. But I can't fathom it. Those men acted like criminals. That's not the way of the police.' He clenched his fist and swore under his breath. 'I'll have those fellows broke for this, if I have to go to Ottawa,' he said. 'And I'm going to run down those deserters, if it takes me a lifetime. I tell you this, Molly: it's all bound up with Joe in some way or other, and Tom Bowyer's at the bottom of it.'

'But first — remember Kitty,' said Molly softly, laying her hand on Wilton's shoulder.

Even the slight touch made him wince, for the pain of his broken arm was becoming unbearable. He realized that in all probability he was in for a long spell of illness. He knew that the bone would have to be reset. His head felt strangely light, and the ground seemed to slope downhill from him in all directions. But he shut his teeth hard, and would not let Molly guess. And a feverish energy took possession of him. He must hold out for the journey, until after the shareholders' meeting — until he had told Kitty!

He flung some fish to the dogs, which caught it, yelping, and then, knowing him to be a stranger, withdrew, snarling at him. They were savage, half-trained brutes, but full of energy. It was likely that they would pull into Clayton early in the afternoon.

'We'll take the police sled and start at once,' he said to Molly. 'It looks as if a storm was brewing. I'll tell Andersen to let those fellows go about noon, and I'll leave the revolver with him.'

Inside the shack, they found the policemen eating their breakfast on the floor, with the caretaker diligently serving them. They were still bound, but their hands were free. They looked up sullenly as Wilton and Molly came back, but said nothing. Wilton handed Andersen the sergeant's revolver, and looked through the equipment on a chair for that of the constable, but could not find it.

'Turn them loose at noon, Andersen,' he said. 'Give them enough slap-bang to carry them on their way.'

Andersen grinned. 'Say, Mr. Carruthers,' he said, 'I guess they've put the lid on themselves all right. You won't need to do it for them.'

'That's about right,' answered Wilton. 'Just turn them loose and see that they haven't any dangerous weapons to do you mischief with.'

'You bet I take care for that,' grinned the Swede.

And, heedless of the stream of profanity which his words occasioned, he filled the policemen's cups with coffee again.

Wilton let Andersen harness the dogs, to save his strength for the journey. The savage brutes snarled at him and seemed inclined to refuse. But Andersen was an old hand. With a few cracks of the whip across the nose of the ringleader, he reduced the pack to sullen obedience. In a few minutes the sled was ready, with the sleigh carrying Joe's body attached behind, and the huskies, harnessed, sitting docile in the snow, awaiting the command to mush.

The sun was just showing above the horizon when Wilton and Molly started on the second stage of their journey to Clayton.

9

The Bitter Cup

There was no riding on this trip, for the dogs required constant attention. It was not difficult to keep them to the road, for the bush on either hand was dense, but they were almost untrained and showed an ugly temper continually, so that Wilton had to ply the whip more than he cared to.

Hardly had they topped the rise behind which the cache was situated when the full force of the wind caught them. A blizzard was sweeping up, and it grew in strength all that morning, until by noon it was almost a hurricane. They pushed on doggedly until about one o'clock, avoiding the temptation to rest at the auxiliary caches which had been established along this part of the road.

The traveling became more and more difficult. Here was rocky ground, with undulating country, the ridges divided by swamps into which the corduroy, roughly laid during the preceding autumn, had already been sucked by the quick-mud underneath, so that they were mired to the knees and buried waist-deep in the overlying snow. It was only by the remorseless use of the quirt that Wilton could get the two vehicles across these stretches.

At one o'clock they came to an empty cache and horse-stable, which had been built in anticipation of winter development work, and had formed the hub of many radiating reconnaissance roads. They had come no more than six miles, and it was still a good fifteen into Clayton. By this time the blizzard had increased to an intense violence, driving great sheets of snow along the road. It was impossible to face such a hurricane any longer.

'We'll have to wait till this lets up a bit, Molly,' said Wilton.

The little shack, hardly more than four walls and a roof, was unoccupied. Wilton broke down the door and went in. He found the key of the stable, unlocked it, and unharnessed the dogs, now whimpering, with their tails against the wind, and quite subdued. He drove them in and shut the door. Then he took the blankets out of the sleigh and went into the shack.

To build a fire was impossible, but they ate biscuit and tinned beef, washing it down with water.

'It'll have to let up soon,' said Wilton. 'If it doesn't, we'll just have to face it again.'

A dozen times he had regretted having yielded to her insistence to accompany him. Traveling in that weather was hard on a man, let alone a girl such as Molly. He looked at her in wonder as he saw her apparent unconcern, the courage with which she faced the difficulties of the journey. But his fears were centered chiefly on Kitty. Suppose he couldn't go on! Suppose he couldn't be at the shareholders' meeting on the morrow!

He had been keeping up with a concentration of will, but he had never felt such pain as radiated from his broken arm. The limb was swollen, too, and the tight bandages seemed to compress the arteries, so that even his finger-tips felt numbed and thickened. And yet he did not dare tell Molly.

Toward the middle of the afternoon the wind seemed to have lessened, though the driven snow still swept in blinding clouds along the road. It might still be possible to reach Clayton soon after nightfall.

'I think we might try again, Molly,' he said.

'I think so, Will,' she answered.

He caught her to him. 'You are the bravest woman I know,' he said, kissing her. 'We must succeed — for Kitty's sake.'

She kissed him back. 'Of course we shall, Will dear,' she answered.

Wilton went into the stable and called the dogs. They were lying with their noses together, and at his entrance sprang to their feet with menacing growls. They knew very well what his advent portended, and it was plain that their wolfish temper was thoroughly aroused.

Wilton had handled a refractory pack once before. He knew that quick action was necessary. Unless the dog element was taught to recognize the mastery of man, the wolf strain would imbue the beasts with its own ferocity. He stepped forward, and, as the gleaming jaws gaped at him, and the animals prepared to spring, snarling and quivering with rage, he brought his whip across the leader's nose with all his strength.

Immediately, with maddened yells, the pack leaped at him. Wilton swung right and left with the whip, and then, retreating till his back was against the wall of the shack, he laid about him with the shortened stock.

The yells of the dogs were furious as the blows got home. The rushes never ceased. With gaping jaws and wicked, bloodshot eyes, the pack came on again and again, leaping at him, tearing at his clothes; one sank its fangs into his right hand, and, as he freed himself with a smashing blow, the others were upon him sideward.

In an instant he was struggling with his one hand against the heavy bodies that bore him back, shielding his throat, thrusting the whipstock into the red, cavernous jaws, while the anguish from his wrenched shoulder almost made him scream with pain.

Everything was swimming round him. They had him down. Their bellowing howls grew fainter in his ears. Mechanically he kept his right hand at his throat. The left, torn from the sling, flopped grotesquely in front of him. He heard the click of the fangs that met in it, and felt no pain. He was swooning.

Suddenly he heard the *snap-snap* of a revolver. A leaping body seemed to stop short in the air, and tumbled on him, knocking him on his face. Dimly he heard the discharge of the weapon again. And then, out of a semi-stupor, Molly's face, and her tears upon his cheeks.

She was kneeling beside him upon the floor of the stable, stanching the blood from his wounds with a strip torn from her petticoat. Upon the floor lay three of the dogs, dead. Two more were writhing and moaning in a distant corner. Wilton looked up.

Molly bowed her face upon his and broke into open weeping. It was the first sign of weakness he had ever seen in her. He held her in his right arm. He saw that his blood had stained her hands, her clothing.

'Molly,' he said weakly, 'Molly — '

She wept in utter hopelessness. 'It is useless, Will,' she sobbed. 'Let us die here. We can't go on. They have torn you. Your arm is broken again. Oh, the snow — the snow — '

She seemed to have completely broken down. She crouched beside him, her whole body shaken by her sobs. And in his apathy it seemed to him good to lie there, with Molly at his side, till he grew stronger, or —

'Molly! Remember Kitty — and Joe!'

His words seemed to galvanize her back to courage. She got up. Her face grew suddenly composed. With streaming eyes she bandaged up his wounds. She improvised another sling, to hold his useless arm.

'I shall walk into Clayton,' she said. 'You must lie in the shack. Help will come by noon tomorrow, perhaps sooner.'

'You're thinking of me, Molly.'

'Of whom else, Wilton?'

'I'm thinking of Joe. I'm going on to Clayton. I'm feeling better. No, listen, Molly! I didn't tell you, but my arm was swollen from the bandages. They had tightened and stopped the circulation. I'm better without them. I'm feeling stronger — and the pain's less. We can go on. We've got to go on.'

'Walk, Will?'

'We'll walk,' said Wilton, rising with great effort. The dying animals had ceased to whimper, and stared at him out of their glazing eyes. Outside the snow was drifting down through the leafless branches, but the wind was dying away. It was late in the afternoon, though no sign of the sun came through the heavy, lowering cloud.

'We'll go on,' said Wilton.

And, going out of the shack, he unfastened the cord of the sleigh that held Joe's body, and took it in his wounded hand.

'Will, it's impossible — '

'It may be. But I'll try. I can't face Kitty otherwise.'

Over the new snow the journeying was not so difficult in their snowshoes, but the drag of the sleigh-rope up the hills and across the corduroys proved almost impossible. Molly and Wilton pulled by turns, sometimes together. Their progress was infinitesimally slow. The night came down and shut them in. And the nightmare of delirium clouded Wilton's brain, peopling the world with phantoms. He lived over again scenes of the past, and always Joe was of them. They chatted and laughed together; they discussed the Missatibi by campfires; they talked of Kitty. It was a night of unmitigated horror to Molly.

And yet the touch of her hand always allayed Wilton's imaginings, and drove the phantoms back to their own realm, and he became conscious of a dual self that toiled at the sleigh, pushing hard uphill, holding it back on slippery declines. The soft snow, though it made the road less arduous, gave less grip to their snowshoes. The weight of it clogged the runners of the sleigh, and sometimes the vehicle would almost sink from sight beneath the yielding corduroy above the muskeg.

And at every cache, at each shack, they

would stop, feeling the sheer impossibility of going on, and sit huddled in their blankets under the lee, with the drifting snow about them.

Yet always they went on again; until at last the never-ending night lifted. The snow ceased to fall; the dun horizon was streaked with fire. And slowly Wilton came back to full consciousness.

They had toiled up their highest hill, and as they reached the summit they saw the sweetest sight that they had ever seen. For far away was Clayton, over the plain, with its ugly streets and bare, new houses, and the gaunt station-buildings, round-houses, and locomotive-shops. And all the plain was flooded with light from the new-risen sun.

They were white as shrouded bodies, besmeared with grime, and Wilton was caked with the blood that had oozed from his wounds and frozen.

'One last try, Molly,' he said, 'and then they can do what they like with me. But it's you who pulled that trick, girl of mine!'

But as he spoke he slipped to the

ground and leaned his shoulders against the sleigh.

'Seven miles yet, and the meeting's at nine,' he said. 'I can't make it, Molly. I've tried. I've fallen short — just short. A little later, Molly, I'll — try again. I'm going to — sleep in the sunshine.'

Molly stooped over him, and it was a harder thing than she had ever done to try to drive the driven man further. But she knew that, having staked all, Wilton would be content with no less than the sacrifice of all.

'Remember Joe, dear,' she said, 'and Kitty.'

He tried to rise to his feet, but could not. Wilton's mind was quite clear, but his body, driven by his will, had collapsed suddenly like a worn-out horse.

10

Power of Attorney

Three horsemen were riding over the plain toward them. They watched them in a dull apathy. Even Molly hardly cared any more, except for Wilton. And he had done all that a man could do.

As the men came nearer it could be seen that they were of the Mounted Police. In the foremost Molly recognized Quain, the inspector who was in command of the detachment at Clayton.

The three trotted their horses up to them, and, catching sight of the coffin upon the sleigh, the inspector dismounted. He looked hard at Wilton, and suddenly he recognized him.

'It's Will Carruthers!' he exclaimed, staring into his face in bewilderment.

Wilton got up with an effort. 'Morning, Jack,' he said wearily. 'Yes, it's I. And here's Miss McDonald. You know her, I think?'

The inspector turned his puzzled glance on the girl. Mechanically his hand went up to his cap in salute. Then he looked at the sleigh again.

'And this is — was Joe Bostock,' said Wilton; and all at once, in the reaction from the nervous tension, he felt the tears streaming down his face, and could hardly keep his lips steady.

'My God!' muttered Quain. 'An accident, Will?'

'Shot!' shouted Wilton. 'Some sneaking bastard's bullet in the bush. Shot at my side! The bullet broke my arm after it had passed through Joe's heart, and his blood and mine were mixed together. It didn't need that for me to know that I'll hound down the murderer if it takes me to my dying day!'

'Joe — Joe dead!' whispered Inspector Quain, half unable to realize it. Joe had been a very living personality in Clayton. 'And murdered!' he added. Then: 'Where are your men?'

'Gone! But they didn't shoot Joe, either by design or accident. That's a story you can learn from Andersen, at the halfway cache.'

'That's where we're bound for,' said Quain. 'We're looking for — '

'And, by the way,' said Wilton with a mirthless laugh, as the relative unimportance of the fact struck him, 'I'm under arrest for having murdered Joe.'

Quain looked at him keenly, and then turned his glance upon Molly in inquiry. It was plain that he thought Wilton was raving.

'That's true,' said Molly. 'A sergeant and a constable from the Pas followed us up to Andersen's and placed Wilton under arrest yesterday morning. They were going to take us both back there, with Joe's body. Wilton wouldn't stand for that, and — well, you'll learn about that from Andersen, too.'

The inspector rubbed his nose in perplexity. 'If Will had told me that I wouldn't have believed him, Miss McDonald,' he said. 'Describe those policemen to me, please.'

'The constable was short and dark, stocky in build. The sergeant was fair, with a long mustache — '

'Bit of a squint?'

'A cast in his left eye. His name is Peters. The other one is named Myers. You know them, then?'

'I do,' said Quain softly. 'Peters is Jim Hackett, and Myers is Tonquay, a half-Frenchman, from the Eastern Townships. They were discharged from the police with ignominy last year after a short time of service, as soon as their records became known, and they got away, taking their uniforms and equipment with them. They're wanted for a cattle-stealing job and impersonating members of the force. I heard that they had been seen in this district, and we were starting out to pick them up. So that ends that trouble, Will. I see you have a government revolver, Miss McDonald?'

'It's Myers',' said the girl, offering it to Quain, who shook his head and indicated to her to keep it. 'I took it!' she cried. 'If I hadn't — if I hadn't — '

And at the memory of the preceding afternoon the girl broke down in tears.

Quain nodded to his men to dismount. 'Get this sleigh in to barracks as quickly as you can,' he said, 'and notify the coroner. I guess a half day's extra leeway won't do that precious pair much good. Miss McDonald — Will, old man, you can manage to ride in, can't you?'

Wilton pulled himself together with a huge effort. 'Jack,' he said, 'there's something I had to do. I can't — I don't seem to remember it very well, but it'll come back to me. It's something — something Joe wanted. Can you fix me up with a drink of something strong if I call at your house?'

'I'll fix you up with a pair of pajamas and a nice hospital cot,' said Quain. 'Great guns, Will, d'you know what you look like with that broken arm? And how the dickens did you maul that hand like that?'

Wilton, staggering to his feet, set his face in a ghastly grin. 'I've held on,' he muttered. 'I guess I can hold on for two hours more. There's a bigger thing behind this than you — or I — know just now. I'm going on ahead. I'm all right, and you won't stop me, Jack?'

★　★　★

Austin Phayre, the president of the Bank of New North Manitoba, stood at the table. He was a man of about fifty, with a gray waxed mustache and gold-rimmed glasses. His manner was pompous, and he was immaculate in his black cutaway, with the expanse of white cuff and tall collar.

'Mr. Chairman,' he said, 'some of us shareholders have requested that the meeting be called in order that we may obtain certain information from those best qualified to impart it, as to the prospects of the Missatibi line, concerning which disquieting rumors are afloat.

'You have before you a statement of our financial position. It is not the most satisfactory one that could be imagined. Of a total capital of five million dollars, nearly one-half has already been disbursed on clearing and grubbing, on surveying, and on the purchase of material that has not yet been freighted in; upon the construction of buildings, section houses, power plant, repair shops, and other facilities at this terminal.

'With the contingencies reserve we have here an investment of something more than three million dollars. The estimate before you provides for nearly two millions more to be distributed over grading, track-laying, water-tanks, telegraph line, bridging, and ballasting. Meanwhile, unexpected difficulties have arisen. They tell us that the entire route will have to be resurveyed; that the swamps are impassable. Operations have been stopped; labor has been laid off, at a heavy loss to us. Some of us are reasonably dissatisfied with this showing. We have a number of questions to ask, but apparently those who are best qualified to answer it are not here.'

He glanced with affected investigation about the table.

'It seems hardly worthwhile to put these questions under present circumstances,' he said. 'But we should like to be informed why the surveyors' reports were not properly checked. We should like to know whether it is going to pay us to build a line out into this unsettled wilderness, and in how many years? We are none of us immortal, gentlemen. And we should like to know whether the route will have to be changed, and whether it can be changed except at a dead loss to our total investment, except for supplies and terminal work. Finally, we wish to elicit the opinion, whether our interests are in the best possible hands.'

'What did your bank invest for, if you feel thataway?' shouted an old roughly dressed man across the table.

'That is exactly what I am trying to find out,' retorted Austin Phayre blandly. 'If Mr. Betts will permit me — '

'I'll tell ye why ye did it!' yelled the old man, rising to his feet and shaking his fist vigorously. 'Ye want to get control for Tom Bowyer, so as he'll have another line to bankrupt. Ye know what we all know, that old Joe Bostock never went back on his friends yet. If he says the line's a going to pay, it's a going to pay.'

Austin Phayre faced him with bland indulgence, twirling his waxed mustache, and ignoring the clamor that rose about him. The chairman tried vainly to intervene.

'We want to know — ' he continued.

'Ye know too damn much now!' yelled

the old man. 'Ye know Joe and Will Carruthers went up to look the line over. Give 'em a chance!'

Jim Betts, a familiar figure in many Western towns since he made a lucky strike in the Cobalt region a few years before, had been one of Joe Bostock's staunchest friends. He had brought in a good many of the investors. Yet now he stood almost alone in championship of his friend. It was true Joe had never yet gone back on anyone who had trusted him. But the new hostility of the Bank of New North Manitoba, indicating the hidden hand of Bowyer, had turned even those who had pledged their faith to Joe.

'If the line ain't no good, what does Tom Bowyer want it for?' yelled the exasperated old man. 'Did ye ever know Bowyer want anything that wouldn't pay? Wait for Joe, boys! Ye won't condemn a man when he ain't here to speak for himself? Ye all know Joe — '

'Damn Joe! I want my money!' shrieked an infuriated investor.

Austin Phayre waited calmly until the hubbub had subsided. 'I move, Mr.

Chairman, that the question of the Missatibi route be submitted to a commission of engineers, to be appointed by the directors,' he said, 'none of whom shall have had any previous affiliations with the Missatibi company.'

'I oppose ye!' shouted Jim Betts. 'I'll fight ye to the end on that. Ain't ye bought every engineer in Manitoba, except Will Carruthers?'

'I beg to second the motion,' said Frank Clark, one of the small investors, and manager of the bank.

Jim Betts threw up his arms dramatically. 'Well, Joe Bostock, ye'd best hurry,' he remarked in a tone of confidential communication. 'Where are ye, boy?'

A noise outside; the door was flung violently open, and Wilton stood in the room. And at the sight of him a sudden, dead silence succeeded the uproar.

He was mud and blood from head to foot. His face, covered with a bristly growth of beard, was white as a specter's, and the skin, drawn tight as parchment over the cheeks, revealed the contour of the bones beneath. Yet it was less his appearance than the look in his eyes that sent a thrill of awe through the assemblage.

Wilton strode to the table and flung down a paper. 'Mr. Bostock's power of attorney, authorizing me to represent his vote,' he said.

He turned to the shareholders, but his eyes sought and held only Austin Phayre's.

'We've been to Big Muskeg!' he cried. 'We've seen it. It can and shall be ballasted and crossed. No loop about it, and no change of route. Only rock, and more rock, till you shall have a permanent way as stable as the New Northern's. I pledge my word — and Joe's.

'I pledge my word that it can and shall be done, gentlemen. We're going ahead to do it. I ask for your vote of confidence.'

Austin Phayre, who had sat down, sprang to his feet again. At first confounded by Wilton's dramatic appearance in the face of intimations, privately conveyed to him, that he might not be there, he had quickly adjusted his mentality to it. The motion must be lost.

And the ringing cheers which greeted Wilton's outburst told him to make a virtue of necessity. Wilton had swayed the meeting. The spirit of success flamed in his flashing eyes and carried conviction in his manner.

'Mr. Chairman,' he said in his suavest tones, 'in view of Mr. Carruthers' positive statement that no change of route will be necessary, of course I am ready not to press my motion. I will substitute a vote of confidence in the present management of the Missatibi company. And, gentlemen — ' He glanced about him and smiled. ' — in order to inspire the public confidence, I ask that it be unanimous.'

'I second that!' shouted Jim Betts, rising enthusiastically. 'Ye snake!' he added in a low hiss that failed to reach Phayre's ears.

Half a minute later the motion was declared carried unanimously, and the shareholders clustered about Wilton. He stood in the midst of them, seeming hardly to see them. His eyes were fixed upon the door, and he was listening for something.

'Where's Joe?' everyone was demanding.

Jim Betts caught Wilton by the shoulder. 'Ye're sick, boy!' he declared. 'What's happened to you? By gosh, his arm's broke! Hold up, boy! He's going to faint!'

Then the door opened quietly, and a girl stood in the entrance. She looked hardly more than a child. She was dressed in black; her fair hair was tumbled about her neck, and her blue eyes were reddened and tear-stained. She glanced uncertainly about her, saw Wilton, and ran to him.

'Joe's dead!' she cried. 'Will — oh, Will!'

A loud cry broke from Phayre. He pushed his way violently through the crowd that had gathered about the two. His face was transformed; his lips were working with rage.

'You heard that?' he shouted convulsively. 'You heard it? Joe Bostock's dead! Joe Bostock's dead! It's a put-up scheme! We've been tricked into voting confidence in him. And he's dead! It's a fraud and a lie! How can a dead man vote?'

The shareholders stared at him. His face was purple, and he seemed near apoplexy.

'Joe Bostock's dead!' he raved. 'And until letters of administration of his estate have been granted, his power of attorney is worth no more than waste paper!'

'Well, say, ain't ye forgetting that the vote was unanimous?' grinned Jim Betts belligerently.

'We'll rescind it! We'll take the vote again! Mr. Chairman, I move — '

'Thirty days' notice of that motion under company laws,' said Betts. 'And I guess we'll have them letters of administration by that time — eh, Will?'

But Wilton, without a word, tumbled at Kitty's feet.

11

An Unexpected Development

For weeks thereafter, he was only faintly conscious of his surroundings at intervals. Once, roused by some injection, he was aware of making a brief deposition for use at the coroner's inquest, and once Molly's face appeared, wet with tears, out of the shadows, and her lips touched him. But he was desperately ill, and it was February before the crisis was past, and he awakened, intensely weak, but conscious, to realize that he was in Kitty's house, and that Kitty had been nursing him.

Feebly he whispered his gratitude, and asked forgiveness because he had not been able to keep his promise to look after Joe.

'You did all that could be done, Will,' she answered. 'It was wonderfully plucky, your bringing him to Molly's house as you did. No one could have done more.'

'And you have saved my life for Joe's sake, Kitty. I'll never be able to repay you. But if it had only been me instead of Joe!'

He was too weak to hide his grief. He looked on Kitty as a sister. He asked for Molly, and learned that she had gone home on the day after he had been brought to the house. She had written often, and a letter had been sent to her that morning, telling her that the crisis was past. Kitty promised to show Wilton Molly's letters when he got better.

'Then you know we are engaged?' asked Wilton.

Kitty smiled a little. 'I couldn't help knowing that,' she answered. 'I'm glad for Molly's sake.'

'I think you should be glad for mine, Kitty.'

'I think she is a very fortunate girl,' said Kitty. 'Even if you are not so rich as some she might have married, at least she will have a husband of her own age, instead of marrying a rich old man to avoid drudgery.'

Something in Kitty's tone made Wilton

look at her in astonishment. She had not meant it, of course; and yet, for the instant, her words had almost seemed to reflect upon Joe.

As if sensing Wilton's feeling, Kitty laughed and reddened. 'Poor Joe!' she said. 'Molly would have been lucky if it had been with him, too. Any girl would.'

Wilton's brow cleared instantly. Afterward came the long, pleasant days of convalescence. All the town came to inquire for him. Among them was Inspector Quain.

Wilton's mind had been all bewilderment as he racked his brains for a clue to Joe's death. Had he been sure it was murder, he could have gone grimly to work on the solution. But there was always the doubt, the paralyzing doubt, that it had been an accident, and that one of the two men who had deserted him had fired the shot.

Yet Bowyer must have known of it; Bowyer had sent the impostors to arrest him; he became more and more convinced that Bowyer had learned of Joe's death that afternoon at the portage, and had devised the arrest to keep him from the meeting. He must have been so sure of success that he had not thought it necessary to spread the news in Clayton, which might have thrown suspicion upon himself.

Quain, who was an old friend of Wilton's, told him that no clue had been discovered. Andersen had released the two ruffians soon after noon, and they had started back toward the portage, vowing vengeance on Wilton. But they had never arrived there, and the only clue to their movements had been the theft of two horses, with saddlery, from a settler thirty miles westward. The inspector had satisfied himself, from statements made by the Indians, that the men had been in the neighborhood of the Indian camp, ten miles away, at the time of Joe's death.

From further examination, he had come to the conclusion that nobody had passed the portage within two hours of the time when the bullet was fired. In short, by elimination, it appeared practically certain that one of the two men had killed Joe by accident.

'I'll pick them up on my northward patrol this month, Will,' said the inspector. 'That seems to me the best chance of a solution. I haven't much doubt Bowyer learned Joe was dead, and planned that fake arrest. But there's no evidence to show he was accessory to the murder. And I don't believe he was.'

Among Wilton's callers was old Jim Betts, to whom he extended his confidence in a large measure. 'Bowyer's guilty as hell,' he declared. 'Phayre mightn't have known. I guess he didn't. But Bowyer knew, when he had Phayre bring that motion forward that Joe wouldn't return. Put that thought in your pipe and smoke it, boy!'

'Jim,' said Wilton, 'I'm giving up my life to the Missatibi, because it was Joe's work. And I'm going to hound down his murderer, if it was murder.'

'Aye, boy, and go cool about it,' counseled Betts. 'It was crafty work, but it'll come out. And you'll find them two snakes, Bowyer and Phayre, under the brushwood. And maybe Clark, too,' he added.

Wilton's impatience both aided and retarded his recovery. It gave him the impulse toward convalescence, but it made him restless. It was the middle of February before he was allowed to leave the house. Nearly two months had been lost, and during that time Bowyer and Phayre, whatever their plans might be, had had a good leeway to develop them.

Bowyer, whose interests were many, seldom visited Clayton, but Phayre had been away for a week after the shareholders' meeting, and Wilton guessed that the two had been in conference.

He resolved to push the work with all his might. Construction of the line northeastward had already been begun, and it should reach Big Muskeg by summer. Wilton had sent word to the subcontractor to complete the camp there, and to engage gangs of laborers in anticipation of his beginning operations in March. Stores had been sent up by dog-sleigh, and the men were already at work.

'Kitty,' said Wilton, 'you know everything is in your hands now. You control the line. And I know that you'll stand by the line to the last, because it was Joe's big dream. He was happier planning to open up these wheat lands to homesteaders than he would have been making millions in other enterprises.'

'Will, you can count on me to the end, for Joe's sake,' said Kitty solemnly. 'And also for yours, Will,' she added, placing her hands on his shoulders and looking earnestly into his face. 'Joe was a very lucky man to have had such a friend as you,' she said.

Wilton was touched by her words; and yet, even in that moment, there flashed through his mind a remnant of the same instinct he had always had, that Kitty had come between them. It was the vaguest fluttering of some jealous feeling, unworthy always, and most of all now Joe was dead. He tried to shake it from his mind.

'I've been thinking a great deal about Big Muskeg, Will,' Kitty continued. 'And I feel my own responsibility. I want to see the work, to know that you are succeeding. And I'm going there to live.'

Wilton was astounded. 'Live at Big

Muskeg?' he cried.

'Until the work is finished. Don't refuse me, Will.' She clasped her hands together in her childish, pleading way that Joe had always found irresistible. 'Joe would have let me. I won't hamper you, Will,' she begged.

'Kitty, you're a trump!' cried Wilton. 'But you can't go there to live. The loneliness would be awful. And there isn't a house anywhere. And besides — '

He did not dare suggest the thought that came to him, that people would gossip about her. He was searching for some way of conveying the idea when he perceived that Kitty's eyes were fixed on his in a singular way. For an instant he felt dimly that it was hers that was the dominating mind, as if the brain behind the pretty, childish forehead was as cool and keen as Joe's.

'It won't be lonely with — with the work, Will,' she answered. 'And I've already made my plans. I'm having a bungalow built there. And I thought it would be a surprise for you,' she pouted.

'It is, Kitty,' said Wilton, staggered by

her well-laid plans. 'If you've done that, it's no use my saying anything more. But you can't live there in March.'

'It won't be finished till the end of April,' answered Kitty triumphantly. 'And by that time it will be warm. And there will be Molly. Don't you want me to come, Will?'

Wilton yielded, and he was glad for one thing: her presence at the portage would mean much to Molly. During the few next days he was in constant consultation with the directors as representing Kitty, who had given him her power of attorney to act for her. He went carefully over the books. He was quite satisfied with their showing. If Big Muskeg could be crossed, the company could remain solvent without increasing its capital.

He devoted his attention to the personnel, taking on new men and weeding out — a thing Joe had hated doing — until he was satisfied that Bowyer had no representatives on the staff.

Wilton and Betts had been named executors in Joe's will. Wilton had already gone through Joe's papers; but this task was much less satisfactory; for Joe, who was a capital director, seemed to have no personal system at all. Everything was in confusion — papers were missing, records mixed up together. Joe had dabbled in foreign as well as Canadian investments, and appeared to have burned his fingers badly in a venture in Mexican oil stock. He had left Kitty two thousand shares in the Missatibi, and a comfortable little capital of about forty thousand dollars, together with the house in Clayton and some property in Winnipeg.

The Missatibi shares, amounting to two million dollars at their par value, represented the bulk of his fortune, and were in a safety-deposit box in the bank's vault. The receipt, however, could not be found.

This was not of much importance, but Wilton went with Kitty to look in Joe's box. Clark, the manager, took them below, opened the vault, and put in the master key. Wilton completed the opening. To his astonishment there were only fifteen hundred shares.

'Five hundred shares are missing,' he

said to the manager.

Clark looked at him in some surprise. 'You are not forgetting that Mr. Bostock hypothecated five hundred shares with us as security for the loan?' he asked.

Wilton looked at Kitty. 'Did you know that Joe borrowed on the security of those shares?' he asked.

Kitty shook her head. Joe had not told her many of the details of his business. And the papers had shown no record of the transaction.

'Mr. Phayre has just come in,' said the manager.

They went up to the president's office. Phayre received them with his suave, half-pompous manner. He showed no sign of remembering his outburst at the meeting, asked them to sit down, and listened to Wilton's statement.

'Mr. Clark, will you get Mr. Bostock's blank transfer of the shares?' he asked.

The paper was brought. The signature appeared perfectly genuine. Joe Bostock had made out a transfer in blank of five hundred shares, in return for a loan of three hundred and fifty thousand dollars, due the 15th of December. Unless the loan were repaid by that date, the control of the Missatibi would swing to the Bowyer interests.

'Mr. Bostock was naturally reticent about his affairs,' suggested Phayre; 'but surely you have found some memorandum of the transaction among his papers?'

'Nothing,' said Wilton. He was almost stunned by the discovery. Joe had spoken as if his control were ironclad.

He went home with Kitty and telephoned to Betts to come. They went through all Joe's papers again. In particular, they scrutinized the checks, in the belief that these might throw some light on the subject. But Joe's methods had been as free and easy as his personality. He had paid out several large sums, aggregating three-quarters of a million, in favor of the Mexican concern, and in other investments.

Even Jim Betts was forced to admit that the transaction appeared regular.

'Jest watch them snakes, boy; that's all,' he counseled. 'Every sound ye hear ain't necessarily them coming out, but when they do come out ye'll hear them fast enough. I don't say Phayre forged Joe's signature and broke into his box, because it's a bigger risk than he's got the nerve to take, but I guess Bowyer wants the Missatibi mighty bad.'

'Once I get the line across Big Muskeg, Jim, it'll be easy to raise enough money to pay off the loan,' said Wilton.

However, he went to see a lawyer, a young Ontario man named Payne, who had set up his shingle in the new town the year before, and had some reputation. He told Payne the whole story.

Payne gave his opinion decisively. 'It's always possible to weave a web out of loose ends, Mr. Carruthers,' he said. 'But it's best to take the simplest view. Mr. Bostock was accidentally shot by your men, and the bank's dealings are not open to suspicion. If I were you I'd put all my energy into the Missatibi, and forget your suspicions.'

That was substantially Jim's advice. Wilton resolved to follow it. However, he arranged with Kitty to have all Joe's papers placed in the safe which held the engineering records, and sent up in it to

Big Muskeg. Only Kitty and he knew the combination.

Kitty had received the news of the loan quite calmly. 'I am certain you will succeed, Will,' she said. 'Once Big Muskeg is crossed, everything will come right.

Two days later Wilton, now completely recovered, started for the bush.

12

Poison

The sub-contractor had practically completed the camp at Big Muskeg, and there was quite a gang of men there, principally engaged in hauling the cut timber. Wilton had taken Andersen from the cache and made him the foreman. The Swede was one of the best foremen in the line's employ, but had fallen from his estate owing to repeated lapses into drunkenness. Joe, who hated to discharge an employee, had given him his job at the cache, and Andersen appeared to have overcome his failing. At least, he had never been seen drunk since his employment there.

Wilton planned to reach Big Muskeg on Saturday night, in order to meet his men on the Sunday, when they would all be in camp. He took a new engineer with him, a young fellow named Digby, who had come with excellent recommendations from an English institute. He was particularly anxious to reach his destination, for he had had no letter from Molly since his recovery. In fact, Wilton had not seen any of Molly's letters to Kitty, who had always in some way evaded his requests. Wilton had ascribed it to a little creditable reluctance to show a personal communication, and had ceased soon to ask her.

They spent the first night at the halfway cache, now in charge of a new man, and arrived at the camp on the second evening, a little after sundown.

To his surprise, Wilton found the camp absolutely empty, though there were plenty of signs of an abundant population. There was nobody in any of the three bunkhouses, with their double tiers of berths; the kitchen was unoccupied and dirty, with piles of enameled plates and cutlery unwashed and scattered upon the table. But snores from one of the benches in the dining-room betrayed the presence of a solitary occupant. A man was lying full length behind the table, his hat tilted over his face.

Wilton shook him to his feet, and disclosed Andersen, dead drunk. The foreman, rudely awakened, stood reeling and blinking at him, displaying no particular emotion except dislike of being aroused out of his slumbers.

'What have you got to say?' demanded Wilton, furious at this lapse on the part of a man whom he had trusted.

'I say — damn poor whisky for a respectable camp!' hiccoughed the Swede.

'Where did you get it?' shouted Wilton, shaking him by the shoulders.

'Over yander,' answered Andersen, jerking his thumb in the direction of the portage.

'Where are the men gone?'

'Over yander,' repeated Andersen, with another jerk.

Wilton strode from the dining-room, his heart burning with indignation. In the morning he would fire Andersen. But who had brought liquor into the camp? It was a thing dreaded by employers of labor, almost more than the occasional typhoid epidemics. While liquor was to be obtained within a radius of five-and-twenty miles, work would be practically suspended.

With Digby at his heels, he strode fiercely out toward the swamp. Big Muskeg was less than three miles away by the new road which had been cut from the camp to the portage. They covered the distance in about half an hour, and struck out across the ice. As they neared the opposite shore they could hear the faint sounds of an uproar in the trading post.

Wilton's heart sank at the thought of the men in the factor's place with Molly. The laborers were chiefly eastern Europeans and Galicians, docile as sheep when sober, but changed by drink into wild beasts. Whoever had brought the liquor into camp should pay for it!

As they gained the opposite bank they heard wild shouts of drunken laughter, and, in a momentary interval, McDonald's angry protest — and then a cry from Molly.

They ran at the top of their speed, Wilton leading. Through the half-open door could be seen the figures of the workmen, assuming the grotesque attitudes of crouching beasts, the bestial faces grimacing in shadows on the walls, and dancing with the flickering candlelights, stuck in the necks of empty bottles.

Wilton burst into the store. It was filled with men, roaring and shouting; they were drinking from their tin pannikins, which they had evidently brought designedly from the cook-house, and filling them from a hogshead of liquor that stood in the center of the room. At the end two men, their arms about each other's necks, swayed in a reel with drunken gravity.

The old factor, wedged in behind the counter, his right arm limp at his side, was pushing his left into the faces of the grinning laborers, and torrents of almost unintelligible imprecation burst from his lips as he tried impotently to force his way toward Molly.

Molly, at the door of her room, her lips parted, her eyes dilated with fear, was surrounded by a ring of men. One of them had his huge paws on her shoulders, and, standing a little behind, was trying to bend her backward toward him.

Wilton took in the scene instantaneously through the thick haze of stinking tobacco-smoke. Everything swam before his eyes. With a hoarse roar of rage he leaped into the center of the crowd, caught the man who had his hands on Molly, and, spinning him round, dashed his fists into his face again and again until he was unrecognizable from the blood that covered his broken features.

Screaming with pain, the man broke from him. Before the astonished Laborers could collect their wits Wilton was in their midst again. He drove them before him; he snatched up a bottle containing a guttered candle-end, and, armed with this terrible weapon, brought it smashing down on their heads till he held only the splinters in his bleeding hands.

Stupefied by this onslaught, the man ran for the door. But, jamming in the entrance, the rear most turned and faced him. Three men set on him, dealing savage kicks, and rushing at him, head down, like battering rams. One caught him in the pit of the stomach and sent him toppling against the counter.

Instantly the whole mob was upon him with knives, screaming with rage. Wilton leaned against the counter, sick and weak for the moment, and unable to defend himself. But suddenly the mob was flung violently away, and he saw Digby, his fists flying like flails, striking out right and left, and felling a man at every blow.

The respite enabled him to regain his feet, snatch up another bottle, and go to the Englishman's assistance. The laborers had no stomach for any more. This time they made the doorway, and ran at the top of their speed toward the portage, leaving Wilton and his assistant panting and exhausted in their wake.

Wilton was about to go back to Molly when suddenly he caught sight of two men who looked like Canadians slinking into the kitchen, which opened upon the side of the store. He recognized them instantly as the two fake policemen, Hackett and Tonquay, and it was evident enough that they had brought the liquor to the portage.

Shouting to Digby, he rushed after them. But they were through the kitchen and had gained the open before he could get within a dozen paces. As Wilton, winded, stopped, Hackett swung round, took deliberate aim at him, and fired.

The bullet whizzed past his head and struck one of the logs of the store building. The outlaw, having hardly stopped to fire, rejoined his companion, and the two disappeared down the trail. It was impossible to catch them, and useless to attempt to follow them with horses.

Wilton went back, breathless, and still giddy from the kick he had received. Digby was waiting at the kitchen door; he had evidently not understood Wilton's shout.

'Good work, what?' he exclaimed. 'D'you have much of this sort, Mr. Carruthers?'

'I don't know,' answered Wilton. 'It'll be part of our business to see that there isn't anymore.'

'It wasn't on our school curriculum,' said the Englishman thoughtfully.

Wilton only glanced at him, and went into the store. The hogshead, overturned in the stampede, was bleeding its life away in slow gulps of water-white liquid. The smell was of cleaning fluid. It was the stuff that blinds and stupefies, a single drink

136

turning a man into his primitive elements. The stench was through the store.

Molly was on her knees before her father, who had sunk into a chair. The old man's face was ashen white, but as Wilton approached, he opened his eyes and glared at him.

'Damn ye!' he hissed with unimaginable fury. 'This is your work! Get out of my store and never let me see your face again!'

He turned, and began to shuffle away, dragging his palsied leg, his right arm dangling. Wilton started toward him, half in remonstrance, partly with the idea of helping the old man to his room. But with a beast-like snarl the factor turned on him and shook his fist with savage menace in his face. Wilton fell back, and McDonald began to make his way upstairs.

Wilton went up to Molly and took her in his arms. The girl was almost hysterical now that the reaction from her fright had come. She lay in his arms limply, and her lips were cold against his own.

'Molly — Molly, dear, it's all right now,' said Wilton anxiously. 'Forgive me! I couldn't have guessed those men would have been wild beasts like that. I thought Andersen could keep them in control. Thank God, I came when I did!'

'You weren't to blame, Will,' sobbed the girl; 'and the men weren't. I don't think they would have done me any harm. I had the revolver in case there was need to use it. It was the sight of you, Will, and the fight — I thought they had stabbed you — '

'I shall be in camp as long as it's open,' answered Wilton. 'Don't be afraid any more. I'll see that no more of this stuff finds its way here. And tomorrow I'll make an example of the worst of them that won't be forgotten.'

He soothed her and soon brought her back to her normal condition. As he grew cooler he began to realize that, as Molly had said, the men were not to blame. In the morning few of them would have more than the vaguest remembrance of the affair. It was the wood alcohol, acting as a physical and moral poison on them.

'How did it happen?' he asked presently. 'And how long have those two outlaws been in the camp?'

'They came here a week ago, Will,' she answered. 'They were very insolent, and said that trouble was coming; they made all sorts of vague threats against you, but they didn't molest us, and it was not till they had gone that I came to the conclusion they had simply come here to see if I had returned, and to spy on your camp. Then I heard that they were peddling whisky among the workmen. Tonight, about sunset, they came in and set down the hogshead on the floor. There was a crowd of men with them, and they said they were going to have a dance. Father tried to drive them out, but they laughed at him. They were quite respectful at first; it was only just before you came that they lost control of themselves. And your foreman, Mr. Andersen, did all he could to get them to go back to camp.'

'Why, I saw him drunk there!' cried Wilton, beginning to boil over again at the recollection.

'He took one drink with the men, and I think that was only to get them to come with him. After that I didn't see him again. But they would have gone when I begged them to, if they hadn't been led by those two men. They seemed to want to make trouble for us.'

'They're here for some object, Molly,' said Wilton. 'It's to hinder the work, of course, but — there's more to it than that.'

'I think they want to frighten us away from the portage, Will,' said Molly. 'Tom Bowyer has been here since I returned.' She put her arm on his as he was about to break into angry exclamations. 'He came about three weeks ago,' she said. 'He had a long talk with my father upstairs. Afterward he came down. I was afraid of him, because he was always boisterous and offensive in his manner to me. But this time he was quite different. He told me that my father was very ill; that he was using his influence to get him pensioned, and that the best thing we could do would be to leave the portage as soon as possible. And he told me he had always been interested in me, and would like to help me.

'I was deceived at first, because I began to think that, after all, he had been an old friend of Father's and that I must not let myself be prejudiced by his business animosities. He wanted me to go to Winnipeg and study stenography, or anything else I chose. He said he would take us both there, and see that my father wanted for nothing. But I told him I couldn't take any steps without consulting you.'

'Good for you, Molly, dear!' said Wilton.

'He hadn't guessed how things were between us, for he changed instantly. He began to threaten me. I never saw a man look so devilish as he did when he knew we were engaged. He swore that I should never marry you, and that he'd drive us from the portage. He went away mad with rage. When those two men came I connected their appearance with him.'

'You were right,' said Wilton. 'But I don't think they'll show their faces here again. And I'll see you every day now. Molly, dear, do you know how much I've wanted a letter from you? Why didn't you write to me?'

She looked up at him earnestly. 'Did you really want to hear from me, Will?' she asked.

'Of course I did. I hoped for a letter every day. Why didn't you write?'

'I wasn't quite sure — you'd want me to,' she answered shyly. 'You see, Will, it — our engagement — came about after I nursed you. And I thought, after you got back to Clayton — I thought — that I'd just wait.'

'You thought that I might change, Molly?' cried Wilton.

She nestled close to him. 'Not really, Will. But I — I don't know, but somehow I — wanted to wait. I hated so to come back here, with you lying so ill, and I was so worried when Kitty didn't answer my letters.'

'Kitty didn't answer you?'

'Only once, when you were nearly out of danger. Perhaps that made me feel that — that I'd better not write to you, Will. But, of course, all her time was taken up with caring for you.'

'She ought to have written you,' said Wilton. 'That doesn't sound like Kitty. And — Molly, dear,' he continued, thinking of Kitty's projected stay at Big Muskeg, 'I've got a surprise for you next

142

month. Just about the thing that would please you best in the world.'

And as she looked at him in inquiry, he drew her into his arms and kissed her again. 'Promise me, dear, that you will never doubt my love for you,' he pleaded.

'I promise, Will,' she answered, looking at him with shining eyes. 'Never — never, dear!'

A light cough at the door startled them. Digby was standing there in an attitude of what might have been called impartial, watchful waiting.

'I'll have to go, Molly,' said Wilton. 'Only until tomorrow, dear. And sleep quietly, because I'll give those men the lesson of their lives in the morning.'

13

Inside Information

Wilton's first act on reaching the shack was to write a letter to Inspector Quain, informing him of the presence of Hackett and Tonquay at the camp, and telling him of their liquor-vending activities. In the morning he sent for Andersen, who appeared disheveled, humble, and repentant.

'I t'ank you send me back to the cache — ' the foreman began.

Wilton struck his fist on his desk. 'No, Andersen, I'm not going to send you back to the cache,' he answered. 'This is a man's job I've given you here, and you're going to live up to it. You'll hold your job, and you'll keep the men under control and see that there's no more whisky peddling around here.'

'By jink, Mr. Carruthers, you yoost bet I will!' cried the Swede. 'I done all I could to drive them two fallers away from here. But what could I do? I can't be everywhere, and I got to sleep sometimes. Last night I took one drink, thinking I'd get the men away quietly, and then — I guess I don't remember no more,' he ended apologetically.

'If you see them around here again, or hear of them, you'll let me know at once,' said Wilton. 'That's all, Andersen. Just try to live up to your job; I don't expect impossibilities. And tell the men I want to see them at ten o'clock.'

At that hour he went out to inspect the laborers, who were lined up outside the cookhouse. They were a dirty, disheveled lot, still showing the traces of the last night's dissipation. Several had their heads tied up with filthy bandages, and one, the man whom he had struck repeatedly, had a broken nose, and both his eyes were closed.

Wilton looked at them grimly. 'Well, men, we've met one another already,' he said. 'I'm your new boss. You've had a taste of me, and you've seen something of my methods. I expect my workers to make good, and I expect to make good myself. I've given you the best camp in the district, and you've made a sty out of it. You'll keep it clean, and you'll live clean. And if any man brings liquor into camp, or sets his foot across the portage without my permission, I'll make him so that his mother wouldn't recognize him. Those of you who are dissatisfied can take your pay and go. How many of you want to stay?'

The laborers muttered sullenly together. Wilton watched them. They scowled and jabbered, and presently a spokesman came forward.

'The men say they'll stay,' he announced. 'They think you're a good boss. You're the sort of boss they like. But they want to go across the portage. They want to find them men that sold them the drink. They want to beat them up.'

'The police will attend to that. They'll have the camp clean by noon, or there'll be more trouble. Tell them to get busy!'

He went back to his shack. Digby, who had stood thoughtfully beside him during this colloquy, came in after him.

'There must be quite a considerable

amount of this sort of thing, Mr. Carruthers?' he inquired.

'What do you mean by 'this sort of thing'?' demanded Wilton sharply.

'Making men so that their mothers won't know them,' answered the engineer. 'It may be all right for those who like it, but it wasn't on my curriculum.'

Wilton put his hand on the man's shoulder. 'Why, you stood by me like a brick last night,' he said.

'Well, I did what I could. But I didn't join your company to be a bruiser. I don't like it. In England, when a man misbehaves, we take out a summons against him.'

'Where'd you serve it?'

'That is a problem,' admitted Digby. 'I've thought over that. But — this sort of thing wasn't what I signed on for. That's all there is to it. If you'd told me what was expected of me, I might have signed with you or I might not. I'd have thought about it. I object to my rights being invaded. So I wish to offer my resignation.'

'All right,' said Wilton shortly. Then, feeling that the other had a sort of justice in his attitude: 'It is rather tough to expect you to do police work,' he acknowledged. 'But I don't think there will be any more of it.'

Digby looked at him in frank astonishment. 'Why, I *like* it!' he said. 'I had the time of my life last night. It's simply the principle of the thing. But I'm afraid I didn't quite make my position clear.'

'Not altogether,' answered Wilton. 'However, I'm sending some special mail down this noon, and you can go in with the sleigh.'

Digby's defection was a serious blow, for it would be necessary to make arrangements for a man to take his place. However, Wilton decided to take no steps to that end immediately. He inspected the camp, saw that a good job was being made of the cleaning up, and went to look at Kitty's house.

This was built substantially of logs, and had already been half completed. It consisted of four rooms and an out-kitchen, and stood at the edge of the new road near the ridge, about five hundred yards from the nearest bunkhouse.

Wilton's shack faced it further down the road, and nearer the camp. He had fitted up one room as an office, and he had arranged to have Joe's papers and the engineering records placed in a strong safe and sent out by sleigh.

That afternoon he made his first examination of the muskeg. He took soundings in several places, but the peat seemed bottomless. Nowhere could he reach rock bottom, except within a few feet of the shore.

He returned greatly discouraged. The swamp was a natural depression between the two lines of bluffs, filled in during the course of uncounted ages, and evidently almost fathomless.

The muskeg was a series of sink-holes, extending in all directions, with the river in the middle, and little lakes ramifying out of it here and there. At the portage the bottom seemed sandy, but this was only drift washed down from above; the underlying bed of peat was everywhere.

Wilton took soundings for several days after Digby's departure, and always with the same lack of results. He went two or three miles up and down the stream without discovering any way of bridging the muskeg.

He was too busy now to see Molly more than an hour daily, but he always went to the portage for a short visit after supper. And he always returned cheered and encouraged with the hope that success would crown his labors on the morrow.

The factor, who had learned to expect his coming at the same hour each day, withdrew upstairs before he arrived. Once or twice, when they came face to face, he turned his head away in sullen anger.

As a prospective father-in-law, McDonald seemed about as hopeless a proposition as could be conceived, but the time to consider his own and Molly's future would not come until the line was on its feet. Big Muskeg was the giant in the way. Often Wilton, staring down at its sullen depths from the top of the ridge, would feel it as a personal enemy, defying him to overcome it.

Meanwhile there was no more trouble with the men. The outlaws had not shown themselves near the camp, and Quain had written that it would be useless to send a party to search for them there. Andersen proved an efficient foreman, and the time was approaching when Wilton must set the laborers to work upon Big Muskeg or lay them off. When the site for the foundations had been located, it would be necessary to drive a fresh road from the camp and prepare new buildings for the locomotives, trucks, and grading-engines that would be hauled up by horses after the snow melted. And the days passed until March was nearly at an end.

One evening Wilton was sitting in his shack, utterly disconsolate. He had sounded nearly every possible place without result, and even Molly had failed to cheer him. He saw no alternative before him except to return to Clayton and confess himself beaten.

Andersen tapped at the door and said that a man wanted to see him. Wilton rose up and, to his surprise, admitted Lee Chambers.

The engineer was roughly dressed and wretched-looking. He told Wilton that he had tramped in from Cold Junction, thirty miles southwestward, the present terminal point of the New Northern.

'I thought maybe you would give me a job,' he said. 'I've left Mr. Bowyer for good. We had some trouble. He wanted me to make a crooked report, and I would not do it. I'm through with him and his dirty schemes.'

Wilton gave him a chair and looked him over coldly. He did not like Chambers, and he suspected that he was lying, and that Bowyer had sent him to him for his own purposes.

Digby's disappearance had left him in a hole, but that hardly justified his taking on Lee Chambers, though he was one of the ablest of his profession in Manitoba.

'Well, Mr. Chambers,' he said, 'I'm carrying on my work here on the lines established by Mr. Bostock. Joe Bostock had two maxims. The first was: 'Never lay off a man if you can help it.' The second was: 'Never take on a man who's left you.' And to be quite frank — I feel about the same way. You left the Missatibi, which had treated you well, and we have reason to believe you gave useful information to Mr. Bowyer.'

'I swear I didn't!' shouted Chambers, springing to his feet. 'Prove that, Mr. Carruthers!'

'I can't prove it,' Wilton admitted. 'I am giving you my personal feeling about yourself, in confidence.'

'Well, it's a mighty poor, sort of confidence,' spluttered the engineer. 'See here, Mr. Carruthers! I guessed you'd give me just about the sort of rotten reception that you have done. Well, I didn't come here to beg you for a job. I want one, and I can get one on any other line in Manitoba. But I want to even things out a little with Tom Bowyer first. He's played me a dirty trick, and I don't take things lying down. I know what your problem is. I know you can't cross Big Muskeg. Suppose I show you, eh? How'd you feel about it then?'

Wilton's cool glance never wavered. 'I'm willing to hear more on the subject, Mr. Chambers,' he said.

'Right! I guess you know why Tom didn't fight Joe Bostock in the Legislature, don't you? He wasn't interested in the Missatibi at first, and he thought if he ever wanted it he could get it. Then they changed the route of the Transcontinental to run north of Height of Land, and that meant that the Missatibi could link up between it and the New Northern without any rock-tunneling worth speaking of.

'That changed the whole aspect of affairs. There was the loose end of a cheap line dangling in Tom Bowyer's face, with immense profits at some time or other. Besides that, the rumor got about that Joe was hiding something up his sleeve. Coal, maybe?'

He shot a keen glance at Wilton as he spoke.

'Or maybe copper. Joe kept that close enough, but Tom's interest was aroused. Before you'd even started to clear the bush I was up here sounding every yard of Big Muskeg clear along both shores. And there's rock bottom within two miles of here. Does that interest you, Mr. Carruthers?'

'It does,' said Wilton frankly.

'If I show it to you — '

'I need an assistant, and you can have the position as long as you want it.'

Lee Chambers grinned. 'That's good enough for me,' he said. 'I'll hold it right along. There won't be any other road would have much use for me after Tom Bowyer finds out what I've done to him.'

Wilton gave Chambers a bed in his shack. The next morning they started out to sound the muskeg. A little more than a mile north of the portage, where the river dwindled to a mere trickle between two lakes in summer, was an uninviting bed of peat, covered with rotten slush; it was one of the few spots where Wilton had not sounded.

'You'll get bottom here,' said Chambers. He swept his arm upward. 'You see, I've figured it out like this: Those ridges are limestone. But the foundation's granite. You've noticed that, of course. The granite was there first. The limestone was forced up later through the clefts by subterranean action. It filled up the holes and hollows and spread up above the granite till these bluffs were formed. But the granite hasn't shifted. Here's where the granite bed extends across the muskeg. The mud filled up the cleft and spread across the foundation. But the foundation's there. Try her out!'

Wilton got bottom after two or three attempts. They spent the day there, crossing to the opposite shore and taking soundings repeatedly. As Chambers had said, here was the foundation for the permanent way — not the best conceivable, and one that would require considerable ballasting, but undeniably the only route possible.

That evening was the happiest that Wilton had ever spent at the portage. Molly was as delighted as he.

'It saves the line,' he said. 'It was a big chance to take, and if I had guessed the difficulty I don't think I would have taken it. But it saves Joe's line. If only he could be here!'

The next day preparations were begun for cutting the new road from the camp. This, in turn, was to link with the original route a few miles back, to avoid more than four degrees of curve. A passage three feet wide was first cleared through the bush, a row of stakes was planted, representing the center of the line between the pair of metals, and the track was then extended to a width of a hundred feet, and grubbed.

The weeks passed swiftly. With mid-April came the breaking up of the ice. The river, unchained from its manacles, disgorged its swollen torrent. The snows melted in a myriad muddy streams. The ground hardened, and the first team of horses struggled into camp, drawing its freight.

There followed the heavy artillery of construction: steam-shovels, pile-drivers, grading-machines, miles of rails, and ever more supplies for the camp's increasing needs. The narrow-gage arrived, the shanties of the station-men began to dot the line at intervals of a hundred feet. The telephone posts extended right to the swamp's edge. With this material came new gangs and foremen, locomotive engineers and mechanics. The whole camp hummed like a hive.

The end of April saw Kitty's house completed and the furniture installed, and the first day of May brought Kitty.

14

The Declaration

She had telephoned Wilton to expect her, and she came in a rig, with a cartload of trunks and packages behind. Within an hour she was ensconced snugly in the new cottage, with a camp cook detailed to look after her needs. In her widow's black she looked prettier than ever, and absurdly young even to be married.

Clothes, hangings, books, feminine things, knickknacks of every kind strewed all the floors as soon as the heavy trunks had been unfastened. For several hours after her arrival there was chaos in the cottage.

Wilton had supper with her, and all the while they sat together at the table his heart was almost too full for speech. He was dreaming of the future with Molly, a future in which Kitty shared. He pictured her happily married — for Joe would have wished that, and Wilton's loyalty to the dead man had nothing mawkish or sentimental in it. He imagined someone altogether worthy of her, and they four the closest of lifelong friends.

Kitty tapped him on the arm, and he looked up to see her face in a charming smile, and mirth dancing in her blue eyes.

'What are you thinking of, Will?' she asked.

'Kitty,' he said, evading her question, 'I think you are the pluckiest woman in the world.'

'Why, Wilton?'

'To come up here and put up with these hardships, just because of Joe.'

She blushed faintly and lowered her eyes. 'It was you who let me come, Will,' she said.

'But you wanted to come because Joe would have liked it, Kitty. It's just like you to hide your real feeling.'

She laughed, and made a little face at him. But after supper she grew serious as he spoke of the work and his success, about which he had written her.

'How glad Joe would have been,' he

said. 'Somehow it seems to me that every stroke of the ax, every blow of the hammer, is part of a great memorial to him.'

That was the nearest to poetry Wilton had ever got. Kitty fell into a meditation as prolonged as Wilton's at the table, until he asked her if she would walk over to the portage to see Molly.

'Tonight?' she asked doubtfully. 'I thought you might be content to sit here and chat.'

'I should be, Kitty. But I told her I was coming. And I said I had a surprise for her. Can't you imagine how pleased she'll be to see you? But if you're tired — it was thoughtless of me, but somehow I can't fancy anyone not wanting to see Molly.'

'Why, of course I'll come with you, Will,' she answered.

And they strolled down side by side and made their way to the trading store. Upstairs the lamp was lit in the factor's room, and as they drew near they could see the old man seated in his chair, and Molly kneeling at his side. She seemed to be pleading with him. Wilton felt hurt and angry at the thought of her position. Somehow he hated Kitty to see that scene.

They went in, and, at the sound of their entrance, Molly came running downstairs, stopped short at the bottom, and stared at Kitty as if she had seen a ghost. She put her hand to her heart with a sudden gesture of fear.

'Molly, this is the surprise I promised you,' said Wilton. 'What's the matter, dear? Did we startle you?'

Molly shook her head, and came quickly forward, swallowing as if something was choking her. The women kissed each other. Then Wilton was aware that both were watching him.

All through the lively chat that followed he was conscious of that. He put the idea out of his mind with an effort, for he did not like subtleties of feeling that he could not understand. Yet there was a chilliness under the girls' chatter and laughter.

Presently Kitty said she was tired and must get back. Molly promised to come to see her as soon as possible. And Wilton was outside with her, and Molly's kiss warm on his lips still, when suddenly the explanation of the slight constraint came to him.

Kitty gave him his opportunity. 'Did you think Molly seemed a little strange?' she asked, with a quick glance at him, and that odd, keen look in her eyes.

'I think she was surprised,' said Wilton. 'And perhaps — I can say it to you, Kitty? — the least bit hurt. She was very anxious about me when I was ill, you know.'

'Why, Wilton!'

'Of course she didn't understand that it was impossible for you to answer her letters immediately.'

'Well, I answered every one!' said Kitty indignantly. 'Did she say I didn't?'

'Of course, they mightn't have reached her. But I didn't mean to offend you, Kitty. It's only a trifle, anyway.'

'I'm not offended,' said Kitty; but they hardly spoke on the way home. When he left her at her door she turned to him and asked abruptly: 'Will, you are still as deeply in love with Molly as ever, aren't you?'

'Of course I am, Kitty,' he answered.

'Then I am glad, for your sake and hers,' answered Kitty, and, went quickly into the house.

Wilton walked back to his shack, a little puzzled and trying to think it all out. He did not like those wrinkles in his mind. He hated things that were not as clear as noonday. Women were queer in little ways, he knew, and apt to make much of trifles. But the two girls were old friends. He was sure the little ripple would pass away.

He had arranged to show Kitty the progress of the work on the following morning; but when he called for her he found her in the midst of her unpacking, and she put it off until the afternoon. Wilton laughed, chided her a little, and went to his work. It had never occurred to her that he was giving up valuable hours of the company's time to the appointment.

And he thought with an inward smile how those same unpractical ways of hers had been at once Joe's despair and his delight. They had been complete contrasts in temperament, a thing which, perhaps, had been the secret of their happiness together. Wilton had quite forgotten the little storm of the night before.

She kept him waiting till three o'clock, when they started. The camp had spread itself like a great wen among the trees. The clang of hammers, the sounds of the various engines was like a great paean in Wilton's ears. It was a paean of Joe; it embodied all the essence of constructive life to him. A man's job!

He felt the pride of the artist as he led Kitty from one place to another. Locomotives were snorting, and lines of ballast trucks occupied the narrow-gage that had been laid down to the water's edge. Here, eating into the debris of the clay, was the grader. A dozen horses, hitched in four rows of three abreast, strained at the great plow that ripped tons of earth from the soil, forcing it into the scoops which, traveling on an endless chain, discharged their contents into the hopper wagon.

Here, in the ballast pit, from which the screech of steam was heard from morn till night, the great, unwieldly steam-shovel scraped its huge steel teeth into the face of the cut with the scrunch of an ogre's feast, and, turning, disgorged its plunder into the empty trucks alongside.

Kitty shuddered, and pressed Wilton's arm. 'It's like — it's like some living monster, Will,' she said. 'Let us go on.'

He led her toward the muskeg. But on the way he stopped suddenly beside the summit of the ridge.

'Kitty,' he said in a low voice, 'I don't know if I ought to tell you — perhaps you'd like to know. This is where Joe — '

Her grasp upon his arm tightened convulsively. 'No, no, Will!' she said hurriedly. 'I don't want to see it; I can't bear to think of it.'

They followed the line of ballast trucks along the narrow-gage down to the swamp's edge. Construction upon the foundations was well underway. Tons of debris had been poured into the muskeg, and had simply spread themselves over the bottom, finding their level like water. Soundings taken had showed the bedrock hardly raised from its level twenty feet beneath the surface.

Wilton and Lee Chambers had therefore begun the construction of trestle-work. Teams hauled bundles of logs, bound with a chain, to the scene of operations. The uprights for the lower tier were driven into the ground, and the horizontal members and diagonals were nailed up, completing a crazy, shaking structure just strong enough to take a pair of metals at the top.

Along this the ballast trucks would groan, to dump their spoil about the feet of the structure, which thus held it together and enabled the muskeg to be filled more rapidly. In places this work was strengthened by a horizontal network of heavy logs, laid upon massive balks of timber, calculated to compress the elastic muskeg to the limit of its capacity and hold back the pressure of the spring ice-jam.

As they reached the edge of this structure the whistle blew. The workmen knocked off and came slowly past them toward the camp. Wilton and Kitty stood alone at the edge of the embankment, where the flimsy structure of the trestle began.

Kitty looked at Wilton breathlessly. Her

her eyes were shining. 'It's wonderful, Will,' she said. 'It makes me feel so out of place and useless.'

There was a little sob in her voice. Wilton looked at her in great surprise. 'Why, how can you feel that way, Kitty?' he asked reproachfully. 'You have been loyal to the core to Joe!'

'Don't say that!' she cried fiercely, and, turning swiftly from him, began to make her passage across the temporary sleepers. Twelve feet beneath them the sluggish stream forced its narrow channel through the muskeg. Wilton called to Kitty.

'You'd better come back,' he shouted. 'It isn't very secure, and you might lose your footing.'

But she went on without heeding him, until she stood almost at the end of the shaking structure. It was a dangerous place. The wind blew strongly, sending her skirts flying about her, and tumbling her hair upon her shoulders.

'Come back, Kitty!' called Wilton, making his way across the planks until he reached her side. He put out his hand to steady her. Then he saw that the tears were streaming down her cheeks.

'Why, Kitty, what is it?' he begged. 'I didn't hurt you?'

She shook his hand from her arm with a violent gesture, leaning back; and suddenly she lost her stance and toppled from the edge of the trestle into the river below.

A plunge into that viscous water was more dangerous than a fall. Wilton realized it instinctively. He leaped feet first, and found himself struggling in the gluey swamp, half mud, half water. Kitty, who had fallen into the center of the stream, appeared half a dozen feet away, her white face upturned, her hands catching for support as the shallow current carried her toward the lake.

Fighting madly, Wilton detached his limbs from the sucking mud and managed to grasp her skirt as she drifted past him. With a desperate effort he drew her to him and struggled through the yielding muskeg until he was able to catch an upright of the trestle-work.

He glanced at Kitty as he halted to catch his breath. She lay passive in his arms, her eyes closed; she seemed to have fainted, but she breathed easily, though quickly. Her dripping clothes clung to her tightly, and her fair hair streamed over his arms.

Then, plodding through the yielding swamp, he struggled on until he reached the shore. He set her down at the edge of the embankment, on the grassy slope of the hill. Kitty opened her eyes and fixed them upon his.

'Thank God, we're all right now!' said Wilton. 'It was a near thing in that muskeg. You lie quiet and rest a little, and then we'll hurry back, and you must change your things quickly.'

There was a quick catch of Kitty's breath. 'Oh, Will, you are so blind!' she whispered. 'Couldn't you see? Are you going to make me tell you, Will? Are you going to make me tell you that I love you?'

She put her arms about his neck, and her face on his shoulder. Wilton, dumfounded, hardly stirred; he did not know what to do.

'I'll tell you, because I see I must,' she

whispered. 'I've always loved you, Will. And I never cared for Joe.'

'Kitty!'

The cry that broke from his lips held all the anguish of his disillusionment. His face grew scarlet. He tried to free himself, but she clung tightly to him.

'You've *made* me tell you, Will, and you must hear me now,' she said. 'I never cared for Joe — not in that way. He wanted me, and I thought I could learn to love him. I was happy with him, but what could he expect? He would have been old enough to have been my father. What right had he to marry me, ignorant as I was of love and of the world? I was happy with him — till I met you.

'I always loved you, Will, and it was my right to love you. It was you built up in your mind all that about my loyalty to Joe. I cared for Joe in a way, but that was all. If you imagined all that you did, was I to blame for it? Sometimes you nearly drove me crazy with your talk about Joe, about his work, about my loyalty to him, when I was hungry for your love.

'I'm ashamed — God knows how I'm

ashamed to tell you this. You made me, Will. While Joe lived I was true to him. I'm free, and you are free, and love cannot be bound. And I don't care a snap of my fingers for the Missatibi. I care for you. I'm shameless now, when I say this, but you should have seen — you should have known. What right had you to drone out your refrain of Joe, Joe, all the day to me, when my heart was crying out for you, and you would not hear it? I want your love, Will! I want you to love me, and to take me away from Manitoba, where I'll never hear of the Missatibi again — or Joe!'

Afterward it seemed to Wilton like a dreadful dream. Gently he put her arms from his neck, and rose to his feet. And, because the nature of the man was of that simplicity that instinctively understands, it was not anger, but a deep pity that filled his heart.

'I'm sorry, Kitty,' he said. 'What you have told me makes an end of much that I have planned and dreamed of. It takes the zest out of things. It was my fault. Let us go back.'

She looked at him with white face, set lips, and blazing eyes. She rose without a word, declining his hand, and without a word they went back along the cleared road in the twilight. He left her at her door.

He went to his shack, and sat at his desk for a whole hour, his head resting heavily in his hands. All that he had given his life to seemed broken, his ideals outraged; his love for Molly was the lodestone of his life, but even love is not all a man has to live for.

After a long time he was aware of a low tapping at his door. He rose and opened it. Kitty stood there in the gathering darkness. She came a few steps into the office, and stopped.

'Will,' she said in a low voice, 'I want to ask you to forget. It was true what I told you — partly true. But I was overwrought and weak.'

The heavy cloud that hung about him partly lifted. Wilton grasped at the hope she gave him as a man, convinced against his will, turns again to his accustomed habits of thought, and will not see.

'Kitty,' he said, 'I should have known. I was blind. I looked for perfection. I was to blame. Let us forget it all.'

She answered in the same strained, monotonous voice. 'I did love Joe,' she said. 'In a way, I did. As much as women mostly love their husbands. I gave him all the love that was his right. And I do care for the line. I want you to wipe all memory of this afternoon out of your mind. Try to think of me as you used to.'

He took her hands in his. 'It's all forgotten, Kitty,' he said. 'We won't think of it again.'

But all that night his thoughts revolved about that dark spot in his mind, which he had barred off, as if it had been a prison.

15

Treachery

When Kitty left the shack, she went slowly toward her house. At the door she hesitated, and then, as if with a sudden resolution, she made her way quickly in the direction of the portage.

There was a rig with two horses before the factor's door. Inside the door Tom Bowyer was standing, and Molly faced him, white to the lips, and rigid.

'I've given you your answer many times,' said Molly.

Bowyer smiled. 'No decision that was ever made can't be changed,' he retorted.

'I'll never change. You've shown yourself in your true colors.'

'You speak as if I were a criminal!' he cried. 'Is it a crime to love you — to want to make you my wife?'

'No; but it is a crime to persecute me

when you know you have not the right to ask me at all.'

Tom Bowyer, who had cultivated his rages until they had mastered him, could never refrain from falling into the bully's pose when he met opposition. He slammed his fist down fiercely on the counter.

'I'll change your answer, Molly!' he cried. 'Before I leave this store tonight. I'll have you at my feet, for all your pride. Damn it, it's your pride I want as much as you. I want to humble you, because there's never been man or woman I couldn't tame sooner or later. I'm making you an honorable proposal. Your father's a dying man. Anyone can see that. I want you, and I want to take care of him for your sake, the rest of his days. I ask you to be my wife, to come to Cold Junction with me and marry me. D'you suppose he could hold his job here another day if the company knew he's paralyzed? I'll drive him from the portage unless you marry me and let him take his pension and live with us.'

'I tell you 'no' again!' cried Molly.

'How many times am I to answer you? Will you go now?'

He caught her by the wrists, thrusting his face forward into hers. 'Why won't you marry me?' he shouted. 'Why? How many girls wouldn't jump at the chance I'm offering you? How many wouldn't be glad enough to take it, with or without the wedding ring?'

'Let go my hands!' cried Molly, struggling furiously. 'You coward! If Will Carruthers were here, you wouldn't dare!'

She screamed in fear, and they heard the dragging footsteps of the factor in his room above. The old man felt his way slowly down the stairs and edged along the counter. There was fear in his sunken eyes; but it was anger made him tremble.

'Ye go too far, Mr. Bowyer!' he quavered. 'Ye canna insult my girl in my own house!'

'Get back to bed, you old fool!' sneered Bowyer. 'Didn't you do your own love-making?'

'If she winna have ye I winna sell her!' cried McDonald in shrill tones. 'She's flesh and blood to me — '

'We know all about that, McDonald!' jeered Bowyer. 'A fine father you are to her!'

'I tell ye I winna sell her!' screamed McDonald furiously. 'Leave the house and do your worst!'

'If I do,' answered Bowyer, 'I'll do it. D'you mean that? Answer me, McDonald!'

The factor sank back against the counter and glared at him with haggard eyes, his gray beard brushing his breast. Bowyer smiled triumphantly.

'Speak for me, McDonald,' he jeered. 'Tell her why she'd better change her mind.'

The factor raised his head. 'Molly, lass,' he whimpered, 'it's a grand opportunity he's offering ye. Have ye no thocht of that? It'll be a hame for ye in my old age, when I canna care for ye.'

Molly fixed her eyes in horror upon McDonald's. But Bowyer strode between them.

'You're a fine love-maker!' he sneered. 'Get out of the way!'

And, inflamed almost to madness, he seized Molly in his arms and pressed his lips to her cheek and throat again and again.

'I guess you're not so coy as you pretend, Molly,' he cried. 'You women are all alike, after all. I never knew one yet that wasn't in a hurry to get hitched up, however much she pretended to dislike it.'

The opening of the door behind him made him start. Kitty stood there, and it was quite clear that she had been a spectator of the scene. With a strangled cry Molly broke from Bowyer's grasp and ran into her room. She dragged her bed against the door and stood behind it, sobbing with terror and anger. The factor leaned against the counter, a look of dull apathy on his face. Bowyer turned sheepishly to Kitty.

'Well, I guess you caught me this time, Mrs. Bostock,' he said. 'But, being a woman, you'll understand.'

Kitty's disgust for Bowyer held her silent. She made the slightest gesture of her head to him and went out of the store. Bowyer followed her.

'What does it mean?' asked Kitty.

'It means that I want Molly McDonald,

and I've never wanted any man or woman yet that I didn't get,' said Bowyer. 'Make the most of it,' he blustered. 'I've as much right as Carruthers, haven't I?'

'No,' said Kitty.

'Why haven't I?'

'Mr. Carruthers was first. They are engaged.'

'By God, what's to stop her breaking it?'

As his agitation subsided, Bowyer, a keen judge, noticed that Kitty's poise was unnatural; she seemed laboring under some suppressed emotion. He looked quickly into her eyes and saw that she had been crying. And then he knew.

A slow smile spread over his face. Kitty Bostock had not made Big Muskeg her home so long out of devotion to the memory of Joe.

Bowyer, who used everyone in some capacity, had often thought of making use of Kitty, but Kitty was one of the few people whom he had not understood, and consequently feared. In some ways Kitty was like a child. In others she was as hard as a man. Bowyer had read her better than Wilton had, and his instinct had been to keep away from her.

With a deliberated impulse he put out his hand and took hers. 'I want two things, Mrs. Bostock,' he said. 'Molly McDonald, and the Missatibi. How many do you want?' He looked at her still more keenly. 'One?'

Kitty said nothing, but there was the slightest nod of her head in answer. She was struggling with her loathing of Bowyer, and with the fascination of the suggestion that had already crept into her mind from his, before he uttered it.

'It's a shame, Mrs. Bostock, that you should have to lose all Joe's money in that ten-cent line,' said Bowyer. He was quite at his ease now, feeling himself in his accustomed element of intrigue. 'Even if it could be built, it wouldn't pay. And if it did pay I'd take it myself. I want it, anyway. Not that I'd hurt you, if I could help it, Mrs. Bostock; but I've got my interests to look out for. Business is a hard game, and a woman can't carry on a line like the Missatibi. Joe couldn't have done it.'

'Well?' asked Kitty, breathing quickly.

'By the end of the year your shares will be worth nothing. You'll be ruined. It will be impossible to raise the capital to keep the line, either. I said it was a shame you should lose all your money, and it's a shame that Carruthers should waste his time and strength trying to carry out an impossible dream. If you could sell your shares at par when the note falls due, you could pull out, and you and he could make a sensible investment. He'd soon get over the disappointment. You could see to that.'

He could not hide the flicker of a smile. Kitty saw it, and loathed Bowyer the more. She knew he was playing on her hopes, and yet the sudden vision made her heart beat furiously.

'I'm going to marry Molly,' he continued. 'I swear that I possess the power to make her my wife. But I want the line in return. I want to see some of Joe's papers. They're yours, and you can let me see them without doing wrong, and you'll be helping Carruthers indirectly. They're in his safe. You know the combination.

'I'll marry her this fall. I can push

things, but I want to use my own methods. I don't want to hound the girl or drive her to do something unexpected. I think it's best to go slow. You can trust me, Mrs. Bostock, because you oversaw just how I feel about her.'

★ ★ ★

Kitty tapped softly at the door of Molly's room. 'He's gone, dear,' she whispered. 'Let me come in to you.'

The bedstead was dragged back. Molly stood before her, white-faced and tense. Kitty put her arm round her and sat down on the bed beside her.

'Tom Bowyer's a beast, Molly,' she said. 'But most men are. If you give them the least bit of encouragement — '

'I never encouraged him!' cried Molly, sobbing violently. 'I've always hated the sight of him. He has some power over Father.'

'He seems very fond of you,' suggested Kitty.

'Do you call that fondness? I hate him. I hate the sight of him.'

Kitty stroked her cheek softly. 'You haven't met very many men, dear. Love doesn't amount to very much. And it doesn't last very long. I was quite happy with Joe, after the first month or two.'

Molly looked at her in wonder. 'Why, I thought you and Joe loved each other!' she exclaimed.

'I admired Joe and I respected him. And then, there was not the dreadful specter of poverty with him. Joe was a man like Will Carruthers; he'd keep his word, no matter at what cost.'

Molly sprang to her feet. 'What are you hinting at?' she cried hysterically. 'What word is Will keeping? Do you mean his promise to me?'

And she thought bitterly of his increasing absences, which she had loyally borne because she knew his heart was in his work.

Kitty drew her down beside her. 'I haven't the right to speak for Will,' she said, 'except that he was Joe's oldest friend, and he's throwing his happiness away because he made a rash promise when he was ill. Can't you see, Molly, dear — Heaven knows how I hate hurting you, but I'm thinking of your happiness as well as Will's — can't you see that it was only a passing episode to him, this engagement?'

Molly sat perfectly silent, fixing her eyes on Kitty's face.

'If he had meant it, wouldn't he have written oftener from Clayton?'

'How long was he ill, then?' cried Molly.

'He was in bed a few days after you left. Of course, he couldn't resume his work till his arm had healed, but he wasn't what you could call ill. At least, he went to the directors' office every day to work on the plans.'

Her blue eyes, tranquil as a child's, looked into Molly's gray ones. Presently Molly laughed. She laughed in helpless mirth, so that it frightened Kitty to watch her. Then she put her arms about her.

'To think I didn't know!' she said. 'I have been blind, haven't I? And I thought that it was you who had ceased to love me.'

'I, Molly, dear? Well — it was pretty

hard, coming here with Will Carruthers and feeling you ought to know, and not daring to speak. But please don't take my word about the man you're engaged to. I feel like a mischief-maker. But I love you, dear, and I like Will, and I do feel he isn't to blame. That's why I came to you. And I've no doubt he's honorable enough to say nothing at all, if you want to — '

'Kitty!' Molly sprang to her feet, quivering with indignation.

Kitty rose. 'I don't know now that I've done right,' she said. 'I hope you won't come to have any feeling against me, dear. Only you didn't seem to understand — well, things. And what I'm saying hasn't anything to do with Mr. Bowyer, if you feel that you don't care for him.'

'Care for that beast?' said Molly.

16

In Pantomime

Day by day the trestling grew, and the embankment appeared about it until the first part was hidden under the permanent way. Thousands of feet of logs had gone into the building. Each day the engine pushed the laden ballast trucks further out upon the creaking, swaying structure. Then the pressure of the lever, tons of debris discharged through the frame of the woodwork, and the engine went snorting back toward the ballast pit, dragging the empty trucks behind it.

Wilton was now at the most trying part of the construction. The trestling had almost reached the opposite shore, and the embankment extended perhaps one-third of the way across. At the end of the trestle, however, there were numerous small sink-holes of uncertain depth, having a bottom level of decomposed rock mixed with earth, which it was impossible, by sounding, to distinguish from actual bedrock. Once or twice small subsidences had occurred, and ballast, deposited apparently on solid rock, was found to have disappeared beneath the swamp the following morning.

This might have been due to either of two causes: the supposed bedrock might have given way beneath it, or the suck of the swamp might have drawn it between the timbers of the trestling, so that it spread, like a fluid, over the bottom.

The latter case would require a strengthening of the trestle. Chambers insisted, however, that the subsidences, which were trifling, were due to the layer of loose rock on top of the permanent bed, and that this extended only a few feet down. Thus by a little re-ballasting a firm foundation could be secured. The two men fought the matter out briskly.

'I'll give way to you,' said Wilton, 'because you've examined the bedrock pretty thoroughly. But if there's another subsidence you'll be responsible.'

They re-ballasted, and the delay proved

slight. The work continued, and Wilton pushed his men hard.

Kitty had gone back to Clayton. She had said that she would return, but Wilton doubted it. He still cherished the hope of friendship, when time had obliterated their joint memory of that afternoon. He could not bear to lose her. She seemed a part of Joe, and he found it hard to shake his mind free of his preconceptions. For the present, however, he recognized that her remaining there would prove an embarrassment.

He sent her back to Clayton with Andersen, who had proved entirely trustworthy since the first night, and was going in on business for him.

And he had very little time to think of Kitty in the critical period that followed. Wilton slept only a few hours nightly. For five days he could not even go to the portage. On the sixth success appeared at hand. The sink-holes had been filled in, and there was not the slightest subsidence of the grade. Andersen returned that night and Wilton went to bed in confidence. Chambers was as confident as he.

On the following morning, as he left his

shack, the workmen came running toward him, jabbering and gesticulating. The foreman, hurrying up behind them, shouted and pointed in excitement in the direction of the muskeg.

When Wilton reached the shore he found that his worst fears had been exceeded.

Two-thirds of the trestle-work had disappeared, including a great stretch of the foundation, over which the locomotives and ballast trucks had passed the day before. The subsidence was seventy or eighty yards in length. The top alone remained above the treacherous swamp, and the rails hung festooned in midair.

Lee Chambers came up to Wilton. 'I guess you were right after all, Mr. Carruthers,' he said. 'That muskeg's like glue; it's sliding all the time over the rotten rock beneath.'

Wilton was raging. He turned fiercely upon him. He did not remember what he said afterward, but the storm passed very quickly.

'I'm sorry, Chambers,' he said, holding out his hand, which the engineer took limply. 'I'm pretty much upset by what's happened. You're not to blame; the fault is absolutely mine.'

Chambers accepted the apology with rather bad grace. Something about his manner, perhaps a suspicion of latent complacency, brought back Wilton's suspicions of him. Yet he realized that these were unfounded. He could not have caused the foundation to subside; besides, his was the blame, as engineer-in-chief.

The whole embankment would have to be reconstructed. As the mere mechanical process of dumping might serve merely to add to the weight superimposed upon the treacherous bottom, Wilton determined to lay down a corduroy over the sink-holes — a mattress of tree-trunks. The depositing of the ballast on this would serve to compress the muskeg and loose rock, making a firm foundation, and the trunks, as they became waterlogged, would harden, increasing the strength of the whole structure as time went by.

But for a few hours he almost abandoned hope. At the best, it meant holding up the construction of the line, for the permanent way was now only a few miles behind, and he dared not start operations on the east shore until he knew whether the muskeg could be spanned.

He spent the morning in his office, writing a report for the directors. The news would reach Clayton as soon as it could be telephoned, but at least he would have another chance. It was too late now to think of changing the route without throwing the company into liquidation. And Kitty held control.

The thought of that strengthened his resolve. He could not bring himself to go to Molly with the despondency upon him, but busied himself that afternoon examining the wreck. It was impossible, however, to come to any positive conclusion as to the cause of the subsidence.

For about a month he had had a strange protégé. One evening Jules Halfhead, the deaf-mute, appeared at the door of his shack, and quickly assumed the care of it. He was nearly always to be found there in Wilton's absence. Sometimes, however, he would betake himself back to the portage, and he was free of the camp, where he ran errands and messages for the engineers, and was the butt of mild practical jokes.

Wilton came to the conclusion, however, that the Muskegon's mind was as acute as any man's, and that his apparent simplicity was nothing but the outward aspect of his infirmity.

When Jules had cooked Wilton's supper that evening he came into the office in a state of excitement. The man had loved the work. He was often to be seen on the trestle, clinging for dear life to a plank as the trucks rumbled past within an inch of his head. When he saw the wreck of the embankment that morning, the foreman said that he had burst into tears. Now he was evidently trying to describe something to Wilton in pantomime; but Wilton could not follow his meaning.

Suddenly he seized a pencil from the desk and, stooping, began to draw a picture of the trestle upon the wall with remarkable skill.

Wilton's interest was at once aroused. 'Yes,' he said, nodding to Jules. 'What about it?'

It was his habit to talk, although the

deaf-mute could not hear his voice. Jules had an instinctive faculty of understanding. He looked at Wilton and nodded back.

He next drew four uprights — the long, heavy trunks of considerable girth that were driven into the ground to support the trestling. Then he made a smudgy line across each. Then he drew a hatchet. He looked up at Wilton in pathetic eagerness, and nodded again.

'You mean that someone tampered with the trestling?' shouted Wilton.

Jules, who had watched his lips, nodded eagerly. But, as he always nodded when he was spoken to, little meaning could be attached to that.

Wilton wondered if that was what he did mean. If the uprights had been tampered with before they were set into the ground, by ax-cuts or otherwise, the weight of the ballast would undoubtedly have broken them. The break would not have been immediately apparent, but the trestling would in such case be practically imposed upon the surface of the swamp, without support. The ballast would have spread over the muskeg, causing the entire structure to subside.

'Who did it?' asked Wilton, speaking slowly and carefully.

Jules, who was still watching him, suddenly turned and, with lightning movements, drew a caricature of Lee Chambers on the woodwork of the wall.

Wilton looked at it and drew in his breath. Then he nodded. Jules nodded in return, smiled, and left the room. Wilton reflected deeply.

If Chambers was a spy of Bowyer's, why had he shown him the bedrock at all? On the other hand, assuming that Wilton must eventually discover it himself, Bowyer might have sent Chambers to make a virtue of a necessity, and to secure a position at the camp, where he could be of service to him.

In any case, Wilton could afford to take no further chances with him. It would serve no purpose to accuse him of having tampered with the trestling. He would give him a post somewhere where he could do no harm, and thus get rid of him.

Fighting down the burning rage in his heart, he went down the road toward the shack which the engineer occupied. This was a reconstructed shed. There was only one room in it, but Chambers had asked to have this rather than share the quarters of the other engineers.

The men were back in the bunkhouses, but the door of the shed was padlocked. Thinking that Chambers might be in the camp, he made his way toward the other quarters. But presently he heard someone calling him, and, turning, saw Andersen running after him.

'Were you looking for Mr. Chambers, sir?' asked the foreman.

'Yes. Where is he?'

'Why, he went back to Clayton this noon, Mr. Carruthers! He said he was going in for you.'

Wilton's suspicions suddenly flamed up. 'The key!' he shouted, pulling at the padlock.

'I guess he took it with him,' said Andersen.

'Have the staples pulled out at once!'

Wilton waited, fuming, until Andersen

reappeared with the tool. The foreman wrenched out the staples, and Wilton burst open the door. As he had expected, the shack was completely empty of all Chambers' belongings.

The two men looked at each other. Slow understanding came into Andersen's face.

'He was a bad yun,' said the Swede. 'I guessed you knew your business, Mr. Carruthers, when you took on Tom Bowyer's right-hand man. It wasn't for me to say nothing.'

'Keep your mouth shut still, Andersen,' said Wilton, slapping him on the shoulder. 'We'll just start working again. And keep your eyes open. Some time we'll get him, and I'll telephone Inspector Quain to pick him up if ever he sees him in Clayton.'

17

The Face at the Window

It was five days since Wilton had been to the portage. He had not meant to see Molly in his despondency, but now the discovery of Chambers' treachery came with an invigorating shock and aroused his fighting instinct against Bowyer.

He took the road across the muskeg. As when he had gone to the store with Kitty, Wilton saw the girl upstairs, at the factor's side. A book was on her knees and a lighted lamp behind her. She was not talking to him, however, but staring out of the window, and yet she did not see Wilton as he came to the door.

At his knock she came downstairs more slowly than usual. When she opened the door to him he saw that she was trembling. Her cheek was icy cold beneath his kiss.

'Come in, Will — I have something to say to you,' she said.

He put his arm about her, and they went into the store together. He could feel that she was trembling all the while.

'What is it, Molly?' he asked, looking into her face and seeing tears in her eyes. 'What is it, dear?'

'I'm afraid that we've both made a mistake, Will,' she answered.

Wilton laughed. Once or twice Molly had questioned his love for her, but he had never had any difficulty in convincing her, in the usual lover's way.

'Molly, dear, I know I have neglected you,' he said penitently. 'But you know that until the work's finished I can't ask you something. And I've been rushing it through, feeling that then I should have the right to.'

'It's not the work, Will,' she said slowly. 'I want you to release me.'

The laughter died on his lips. He put his hands upon her shoulders and turned her toward him. She raised her face; her lips were quivering, and the tears had fallen, leaving her eyes hard and bright.

'You mean that, Molly?' asked Wilton gravely.

'Every word, Will.'

'Why?'

'I have ceased to care for you.'

She was keeping control of herself with a strong effort, and she shook more violently. She had nerved herself to offer an explanation, but now, face to face with him, she could not tell him that she had been moved by pity for him, and self-deceived. It was impossible for her to lie to Wilton.

'Molly — ' She saw that his face was set hard as on that night of the riot. ' — I don't play with love. I love you and trust you. If you mean that, tell me again, and that will be enough for me.'

'I — meant it! Oh, can't you understand that I have changed?' she cried desperately. 'I can never care for you, Wilton!'

He released her and turned away. 'Good night, Molly,' he said.

Yet he went slowly out of the door, and, because the shock had come with stunning force, he was amazed that she did not call him back. He could not make himself understood that all his dreams and hopes of five minutes before were broken. Not until he had reached the portage. Then he stopped and looked back. The door of the store was closed. The light still burned in the factor's room, and he saw Molly cross toward him and fling herself on her knees beside him.

He clenched his fists; but somehow the violence that relieved his feelings usually seemed to have no place here. He couldn't understand. He went home slowly across the portage.

The factor looked up when Molly entered, and was astonished to see the tears upon her face. When she kneeled down he put his hand clumsily upon her hair.

'What has happened, lass?' he asked. 'Was it Will Carruthers ye quarreled with?'

'He will never come here again,' said Molly.

A dull fire burned in the factor's eyes. He seemed to be struggling between two impulses: One was to comfort his daughter; the other, his gratification.

'Ah, weel, lass, ye'll find another,' he said.

But he abased his head before her

indignant glance. At that moment the girl felt that her father and she were further apart than they had ever been.

★　★　★

When Wilton reached his shack he took off his coat and flung himself down on his bed. He would not speculate on Molly's motives. He would not think of her at all. He would neither condemn her nor pity himself. A long time afterward — yes; but, under a blow, he pulled himself together and shut his mind as resolutely as he clenched his teeth in determination.

He forced his mind back to his task. The trestle — he would lay down a corduroy — he would drive the men all the summer, if need be, for Joe's sake. Poor Joe! The presence of the dead man seemed to fill the camp just as of old. Joe was the guiding spirit of this work. He had loved Joe more truly than it seemed possible to love any woman.

He completed the few routine duties of the office and went to bed. He had dozed off to sleep when something made him start up in bed and listen intently. He thought he had heard a slight sound in the office.

It was so slight that even his trained ears sent the message to his brain doubtfully. But it came again. Someone had very softly clicked back the catch of one of the windows.

He had the sense of a listener beneath it, and, all alert, Wilton crept noiselessly to his feet and stood listening in the darkness. Now there was no doubt. The window was being pushed very softly open. It was the window between the safe and his bedroom door. In the moonlight Wilton could see that it was opening by inches.

His own door was slightly ajar, and, inch by inch, he pushed it open, too. He saw a pair of hands, white, not work-roughened, placed against the bottom of the window-frame. A face appeared, and was thrust cautiously inside the room in reconnaissance. Wilton recognized Lee Chambers.

Satisfied, apparently, that Wilton was asleep in the next room, Chambers began to climb over the sill. Wilton waited till he was balanced there, and then, leaping forward, he drove his fist with all his force into his face. He felt the bone of the nose smash under his hand.

With a muffled cry Lee Chambers flung up his hands, slipped backward, and fell. As Wilton ran to the window the ex-engineer leaped up and raced toward the trees. The thought of his treachery came into Wilton's mind, and turned his sardonic humor into red rage. He reached into his desk drawer and pulled out the loaded revolver which he kept there. But by the time he was at the window again Chambers was gone.

18

Carruthers is Tempted

Three months later an engine pushed two ballast trucks from the west to the east shore of Big Muskeg. The swamp was spanned. The corduroy had been laid upon the sink-holes, and had borne the ballasting. The trestling ran from bank to bank, and carried the metals firmly, but the foundation was only as yet laid halfway, and the final proof had yet to be made.

However, Wilton had no doubts of the result. He had tried out the danger-spots. The trestle would contain the ballast. His work had been accomplished.

After the subsidence he had paid a flying visit to Clayton. He had not seen Kitty, and Kitty had not returned to the camp, but he had had a stormy meeting with the directors, and, as he had foreseen, had been given his chance to try once more. There was, indeed, nothing else to be done. Bowyer had made the most of the disaster; but it was to Bowyer's interest that Wilton should try again and fail. That would put the Missatibi promptly into liquidation.

Now Wilton had succeeded. Big Muskeg was conquered, and on the east shore the vanguard of the line was driving the cleared way forward and pegging out the way for the metals. Soon grading would begin, Wilton's camp would shrink, and the engines would be moved ahead, and — he would have time to think.

He dreaded that. He had not seen Molly or the factor since that night of the subsidence. He knew that Bowyer had paid more than one visit to the store, but he shrugged his shoulders and put it out of his mind.

He had that faculty. Soft-hearted, like his breed of virile men, he had learned to take life as it came. Adversity braced him. He set his shoulders against misfortune. He would have thought it as cowardly to whine mentally as to cringe before a physical threat.

The workmen, after their months of

arduous labor, had begun to grow slack. There was restiveness in the camp. Once or twice Wilton had seen signs of liquor. He detected it in the slowing up of work; he had smelled it in the bunkhouses — the penetrating odor of cheap alcohol, with its suggestion of gasoline.

Andersen, forestalling him, came to him about the time of this discovery. 'They're getting that rot-gut again, Mr. Carruthers,' he said. 'I don't know where. I'm keeping my eyes peeled, but I ain't said nothing.'

'The best policy,' said Wilton. 'The men have worked hard. When this job's finished we'll let them slack up for a day or two. Then we'll get down to business on this proposition. But if you find out anything let me know at once.'

A few days later came the spanning of the swamp. On the same afternoon a summons came from the court, together with a letter from Quain. The police had at last picked up Papillon and Passepartout, and had recovered the rifle and transit compass. Wilton was wanted in Clayton to give evidence against the men.

The call was opportune. Wilton had already determined to put into execution a plan that he had formed. It was now October, and little more than two months remained before the loan would be called. That would give Bowyer the control of the Missatibi. Driven by the ironical realization that he was working for Bowyer, Wilton had resolved to go to Clayton as soon as the trestling was completed, and try to raise the money to pay Phayre, who, he knew, would not renew the note.

By this time, thanks to a good press, Bowyer had succeeded in making the Missatibi the joke of Manitoba. In the most obscure newspapers Wilton would read of young couples starting for Big Muskeg on honeymoon trips, and arriving with patriarchal families. They dined off snails, and the only freight appeared to be tortoise-shell.

But Big Muskeg was spanned. And, on the strength of that, Wilton believed the time had come to give Joe's secret to the world. He would publish far and wide the secret of the wheat lands. He would establish sufficient confidence in the line to make the raising of a loan a possibility.

Before leaving he placed a night guard on duty over the office, and arranged with Andersen to have three or four reliable men on watch in the event of the laborers attempting to cross the portage. He went to Clayton and laid his statement before a directors' meeting. They heard him in frigid silence.

'That's an old story,' said Curtis, the vice president, when he had finished.

An angry wrangle followed, which led nowhere. They flatly refused to spend any money on advertising. All the while, Phayre, leaning back in his chair, looked on and took no part in the proceedings.

'It comes to this,' said Curtis finally, thumping the table energetically. 'We'll have to increase our capital. The delay has eaten into our reserves. We'll have to push straight toward our objective, the Transcontinental. Then we'll have the monopoly of a steady freighting business.'

He could not get them to listen to the story of the wheat lands. Wilton wanted to advertise it widely, to open it up to homesteaders. He had plans for elevators. But the directors, who resented Kitty's control, were dead against him, and he got no thanks for what he had done.

The following morning the *Sentinel* — Phayre's paper — came out with a cartoon showing a widow dropping her mite into a bottomless pail marked 'Missatibi,' which boiled over a slow fire of wheat stocks.

The story had been known for weeks. It was the joke of Clayton. Several people whom Carruthers met attempted to open it up, until a glance at his face checked them.

Somebody had betrayed the secret, thus forewarning Bowyer and enabling him to open his campaign to deride it. But Wilton would not open his mind to suspicion.

He took counsel with Jim Betts. The old man was frankly pessimistic.

'It looks to me,' he ruminated, 'as if them two snakes'll get the line. Joe must have been mad, or mighty hard put, when he hypothecated them shares.' He turned to Wilton. 'What d'ye want to worry about it for, anyway?' he asked. 'If Joe took a chance like that, he couldn't have felt too strong about it.'

He laid his hand on Wilton's shoulder. 'Whisky's good,' he said in his odd way. 'So's ginger pop. But the mixture's hell. So's women and business, boy. I'd help ye with that loan if I could see my way. But I can't. I've been stung too bad already, and I've got a grandson to look after. Ye'd better make terms with Phayre.'

This was one of the worst blows that had fallen. If Betts had lost faith, who would have kept it? He understood the allusion to Kitty. Betts thought he was in love with her. Then so must other people.

He was due at the court that day, and gave his evidence. The two men received each six months in the penitentiary — a light sentence, on the jury's recommendation. Afterward Wilton had a talk with Quain.

The two men had sullenly refused to give any reason for their flight. If the outlaw Hackett had advised them, they did not put in that plea.

The jury had believed that one of them

had accidentally shot Joe, and that this had been the cause of their disappearance. So did Quain, apparently.

'I'm afraid, Will, that we can't hope for anything fresh upon that subject,' he said.

This business done, Wilton went to see Kitty, swallowing his pride. After all, it was for Joe that he was pleading. Kitty received him in the old friendly manner, with a touch of reserve that should have put him on his guard. But he began eagerly.

'Kitty,' he said, 'you know we've crossed the muskeg.'

Then Kitty showed her claws. 'I was so glad when I heard of it, Will,' she said. 'You've been trying to do that all the summer, haven't you?'

'Why — yes, of course,' said Wilton, looking at her in astonishment.

She put her hand on his arm with a caressing gesture. 'Do tell me what a muskeg is, Will,' she said. 'I've heard you speak of it so often, and I can never remember the meaning of those words.'

And with that the last of Wilton's illusions fell from him, leaving him face to face with stark reality. He faced Kitty very gently.

'Kitty, listen to me now,' he said. 'I've been in this game for Joe — and for you. When Joe died I saw that we'd have to fight hard to keep the line. I saw a lot of money in it, later, and meanwhile you'd have enough to live on, so that we could use your capital and your control to carry out Joe's plans.'

'Yes, Will,' said Kitty, with the air of one who listens wearily to a lesson.

'Joe's borrowing on those shares has changed everything. The loan has to be repaid before the year is out. If it isn't, you lose the line. They'll wreck it, and they'll wreck your fortune, and that of the other investors. Then they'll reconstruct. When the line has ceased to have any value at all, Bowyer and Phayre will have a new line of their own. Do you understand?'

'I'm trying to, Will,' said Kitty. 'But what do you want me to do?'

'I'm proposing this for your sake, Kitty. If you sell your property in Winnipeg you can raise three or four hundred thousand.

I believe I could borrow the rest. That will meet Phayre's loan, and you'll hold the line. It's the only way, because no bank would lend you money on the rest of your shares now, after Bowyer's campaign against us. And he's made the most of the subsidence. It's speculative — what I'm suggesting. But Joe would have done it. And in a few years it'll mean millions.'

'Are you sure, Will?' asked Kitty eagerly.

'Not sure, Kitty, but nearly sure.'

'Will, you are Joe's executor. Do you advise me to take that risk?'

'No!' said Wilton sharply.

'But you just said — '

'As Joe's executor, I can't. It's not sound business. An executor dares not advise throwing away a certainty for a speculation. As Joe's executor — no!'

'Then why did you advise me to?' asked Kitty innocently.

'Because I thought you cared for the line, Kitty. Because I thought you shared Joe's dream for the future of the Missatibi. I thought that, even if you lost, you'd have your house here, and your forty thousand, and you'd feel — that you'd done what Joe would have wanted. As your executor I say, sell out to Phayre before it's too late. At least — at least — '

He could get no further. Kitty looked up into his face. 'Will, I know how you feel,' she said softly. 'I'm so sorry. I've done what you wanted, Will. But I haven't done it for Joe. I've done it for you, Will, you've made your own obstacles. You've never understood me. It's you I want to help; it's you I want my money for, Will.'

Afterward Wilton could not imagine how he had found strength to resist her. With Molly lost, Jim Betts himself counseling surrender, and Kitty caring nothing for the line, why did he not let it go? In that black hour the temptation of her presence, the human love that was his for the taking, screamed their weak counsel in his ears.

It may have been the fiber of Puritan ancestors, or simply the inborn instinct to fight to the end, that gave him his strength. But he did not know how he left her till he found himself in the street.

He went to the bank, the last place, and the last, hopeless effort, foredoomed to failure. He went into Phayre's office.

'Good morning, Mr. Carruthers,' said the president. 'What can I do for you?'

'Big Muskeg's bridged,' said Wilton. 'That should send up the value of the shares. I suggest that you renew Mr. Bostock's loan when it falls due.'

'My dear Mr. Carruthers, that's a queer proposition to make to me!' said Phayre. 'You're not a simpleton. Need I say anything more?'

'You know the collateral is good.'

'Good? It's splendid! I only wish all our paper was as reliable.'

'Well? Other banks may think the same — '

'But they won't,' said Phayre, smiling. 'In ten years, when those wheat lands are in bearing, this will be the newest granary of Canada. Only, they don't know it.'

'How do you know it, then?'

Phayre chuckled and began to drum his fingers on the desk. 'You pledged your word to the directors,' he answered. 'Of course, there were rumors of it before. But your word is good enough for me, Mr. Carruthers. I'm a booster for

Clayton. I believe in those wheat fields — and I'm going to have them. Better throw up your job, Carruthers, and take one with us. What do you say?'

'I'm going back to work for you and Mr. Bowyer right away,' said Wilton. 'At least, I guess it looks like coming to that. But I've got my job to finish — and I'm going to do it.'

19

The Abysmal Depths

Molly did not see Bowyer for two months after Kitty's departure. His next visit was as unexpected as all of his. It was in the afternoon, and the girl came back from a walk along the shore to see him seated in the store, sleek, red, and self-satisfied, and her father standing beside him, with that look of awful fear on his face. She had a momentary impression as if the factor stood up like a well man; but, as she entered, the right leg went dragging under him, and the arm fell limp at his side.

'How d'ye do, Miss McDonald!' called Bowyer. 'I just dropped in to have a chat with the factor in passing. Big things happening here, eh? The Missatibi's mighty slow in crossing Big Muskeg.'

Molly flamed at the insult to Wilton. She looked at her father, and the expression on his face went to her heart. She turned swiftly to Bowyer.

'I don't want you to come here again,' she said. He started up, spluttering. 'We don't want you,' she continued. 'And we won't be persecuted by you. There's law in this country.'

He burst into mocking laughter. 'You never spoke a truer word. Miss McDonald!' he cried. 'I came here as a friend.'

'You can go as an enemy!' she retorted. 'And you can go now. And remember — there are men about here who can use a whip!'

He glared at her, but went without a word, and Molly ran to the factor. 'He's torturing you!' she sobbed. 'I don't know what his power over you is, but he mustn't come here again!'

★　★　★

A few days later Bowyer went in to Clayton, and by chance his visit coincided with Wilton's.

When Wilton left her house, Kitty sank down into a chair, clasping and unclasping her fingers nervously. Her face was white. The first time when Wilton had repulsed her, she had been too humiliated and conscience-stricken to bear him resentment. Her visit to Molly had been a sudden evil impulse, which, when done, she had attempted to justify.

She had, of course, succeeded. Gradually she had begun to look upon herself as a deeply wronged woman. When a woman loves, love is its own justification for acts done in its name. On the second occasion of her advances to Wilton she saw by instinct that she had almost conquered. She saw, too, that, having lost, she had lost forever. She might win Wilton yet, but never in that way.

Now she would go to any lengths to oust Molly. Molly had never written to her since her departure, and she did not even know if her scheme had succeeded in estranging her from Wilton. But she inferred success from Wilton's bearing. He had not looked like a successful lover.

Bitterly she reflected on her marriage with Joe. She had never loved Joe, but neither had she hated him. She had accepted him as an alternative to drudgery, and had been happy, because she had never loved — until Wilton awakened her. It was this unconscious sensing of Kitty's feelings toward him that had been at the bottom of Wilton's slight dislike of her.

She had loved Wilton, and, bound by tradition and social circumstances, she had concealed it. Then — Joe had died. Everything had seemed possible. And Wilton had engaged himself to another — to her best friend. Kitty was not a bad woman, but she meant to fight for her own. From the moment when Wilton repulsed her the second time she had no conscience in the matter. She would win him, cost what it might.

When, therefore, late on the day after he had called on her, the maid announced Tom Bowyer, who had never been in her house before, she sent down word that she would receive him.

She had known Bowyer slightly. Joe and he had preserved a decent courtesy, as befitted business rivals. If Joe would never have had Bowyer in his house, it was because of his reputation, not because of their feud. Bowyer was not received in any decent home.

Neither Wilton nor Bowyer was aware that the other was in Clayton when Bowyer called, nor did they meet.

Kitty came downstairs, to find Bowyer standing in the parlor, twirling his hat in his hands. There was a singularly vulpine look on the red face. For an instant Kitty shuddered inwardly. Her passion for Wilton was taking her into unrelished companionships.

She asked him to sit down. 'I'm pleased to see you, Mr. Bowyer,' she said. 'It was very good of you to call.'

Bowyer uttered a short laugh. 'I'm not a *calling* man, Mrs. Bostock,' he said, 'and the ladies don't like me. They know too much about me.'

'That's very poor taste on their part,' said Kitty.

'That's as may be. I came here on business.'

'I'm glad to see you on business, then,' said Kitty.

Bowyer looked at her in admiration. 'I see we understand each other,' he said.

'That's what I like. You ought to have been a man. Not but what you'd have been spoiled if you had been,' he added, with a clumsy effort at a compliment.

Kitty laughed outright. 'Now I know you have come to get something,' she said.

'Not exactly. We've fixed things so that you'll be able to pull out about Christmas with your full investment. But suppose Carruthers makes trouble? Remember, you've done what you did for his sake as well as your own. You want to help him go into a more remunerative investment. You know that little affair of his is off?'

She started violently, and Bowyer did not need to await her answer. And Kitty could not find words with which to answer. She sat facing him, breathing quickly, her face quite white.

'That's what I came to tell you,' said Bowyer. 'So I know we can count on you to smooth things over if Carruthers begins to wonder. You're staunch, then?'

'You can count on me, Mr. Bowyer,' answered Kitty, loathing herself and him. 'But how about yourself? I understand from you that you were going slow. I hope you're not going too slow?'

'I'm going to speed things up soon,' he answered, frowning. 'What's happened helps things along. I don't know what the trouble was. I thought at first it was one of those lovers' quarrels. But it's lasted.' His face grew red. 'I went there,' he said thickly. 'She wouldn't have anything to say to me. Ordered me off the place.'

'But you were going to marry her this fall,' said Kitty caustically.

Bowyer leaned forward confidentially. 'See here, Mrs. Bostock,' he said. 'If I get her out of the way — if I guarantee that Will Carruthers and she won't meet again, how'll that suit you?'

'You've changed your mind about marrying?'

'Maybe yes. Maybe no. I'm not a marrying man. Nobody is. It's generally an accident — or a trap. But I can promise you there'll be no trouble from that quarter. Also, that she'll be out of the district before winter.'

'That won't do,' said Kitty with sudden fierceness. 'She may come back.'

'She won't. And if she did, and went

down on her knees to him, he wouldn't look at her.'

'What do you mean?' asked Kitty breathlessly.

Bowyer leaned forward again and whispered in her ear. Kitty was as pale as death. 'How'll that do for you?' he asked triumphantly.

Kitty rose, trembling. 'I'll stick to my word,' she said. 'But you're the lowest cur I've ever known, Tom Bowyer, and I hope — I hope somebody flays you — flays the skin off you before you've run your course.'

'I'll take my chance of that,' grinned Bowyer as he rose.

Kitty sank back in her chair, her hands over her face. All of a sudden, the abysmal depths of sin had opened beneath her. She was tempted to run after him and call him back. But she could not stir. It was some time before she forced herself to rise. She went to the window. She guessed that Bowyer was going to the bank. He would return that way, and she could call him in and tell him that she had changed her mind.

Suddenly she started back behind the curtains. Wilton was passing on the other side of the road. He held his head high, yet he walked like a man who was broken.

Kitty watched him go by. Her heart was full of pity for him, for his quixotic dreams, his foolish faithfulness to Joe. The picture that Bowyer had limned of Molly faded from her mind under the brighter glow that came into it.

*   *   *

Like Wilton, Bowyer had business to transact with Phayre. He went to the bank; it was after hours, but he knew Phayre would be there, awaiting him. He went straight to the office. Phayre closed the door behind him, and they pulled their chairs up together.

'Carruthers is in town,' said the bank president.

'He is, eh?' asked Bowyer, darting a keen glance at him. 'When did he get in?'

'Day before yesterday. He was subpoenaed on that case.'

'That's so, of course,' said Bowyer. 'What did they get?'

'Six months apiece.'

'No new light on the murder of our friend?'

'Nothing. Quain didn't go into that phase of the affair at all. He'd questioned them, and couldn't prove anything. The jury believed that was why the men ran away, that it had been an accident.'

Bowyer fell into a brown study for a few moments. 'Carruthers been here yet?' he inquired presently.

'Not yet. He's trying to raise a cool half-million in town. I guess he's been to the last likely place by now. So he'll be here tomorrow to renew the loan.'

'You'll renew, of course,' said Bowyer. 'Excellent wheat lands! Fine investment for your bank, the Missatibi! By the way, you hit it strong with that cartoon!'

They both laughed, first at the cartoon, then at Bowyer's raillery.

'No more trouble with Clark?' asked Bowyer.

'Not at present. I guess that extra two hundred squared him. He's a dangerous customer to handle, though. And absolutely indispensable for a job like we had to handle. A first-class man at his trade, cool as a cucumber, and looking like a gentleman. You'll find it hard to beat that combination. He could have had more than the two hundred he held me up for.'

'He's certainly worth it,' admitted Bowyer. 'What'll you do with him next year?'

'Why, he seems to like the work here,' answered Phayre, laughing. 'I'll keep him on, under my eye — at a reduced salary.'

They both chuckled over that, but Bowyer grew serious quickly. 'Well, I've fixed Kitty Bostock,' he said. 'Lord, it's a cinch handling that type of woman. Once they fancy some particular man, they'll go through hell to get him.'

'You've told her you'll buy her shares at par,' Phayre said sharply. 'You haven't committed yourself irrevocably to that?'

Bowyer threw his head back and emitted one of his short laughs. 'Well, I may change my mind,' he said. 'It isn't in writing.'

'Suppose she raises Cain?'

'She can't. She's in too deep. She doesn't know how deep.'

Phayre laughed again, but nervously. 'I never cared much for this business, Bowyer,' he said. 'If Joe Bostock hadn't died as he did I'd never have got mixed up with it. But that gave us our chance. It was a very lucky accident. If we weren't committed beyond recovery, I'd pull out even now.'

'Pull out?' echoed the other. 'How the devil can we pull out? The trick's done.'

'You've — '

'I've fixed it about that safe. We had a devil of a job the first time we tried. He's got a deaf-mute there who seems to have eyes like a cat, and sleeps with them open. Carruthers caught Lee Chambers at the window and smashed his nose. And, of course, Chambers' usefulness at the camp is ended. However, I've fixed it now, and a day or two will see us with what we want, and Carruthers with what he doesn't want.'

'I wish you luck,' said Phayre.

'Wish yourself luck, too. The whole plan's perfect, Phayre, so you can get out that old kit bag and stow your troubles away in it.'

'I suppose there's no doubt Passepartout and Papillon did kill Joe Bostock,' suggested Phayre, darting a keen look at the other.

'I guess not,' answered Bowyer. 'Anyway, it's no business of ours how it happened. Quain put everybody through the mill, including me.'

'And me,' said Phayre.

'That shows he's at his wits' end. If a new clue comes to hand he'll jump at it, for the sake of his reputation. By the way, Quain's the man I came in to see you about. You've had a talk with him?'

'I saw him yesterday.'

'How did he take it?'

'Fine!' said Phayre, rubbing his hands. 'Hook, bait, and sinker. I could see the flash of illumination come into his eye as the seed began to sprout. Of course, he was quite noncommittal outwardly.'

'You didn't suggest — ?'

'No; I'm not quite such a fool as that, Bowyer. I spoke to him about Joe Bostock's investments, and the missing half-million that he had drawn out a day or two before his murder. And I left Quain to draw his own inferences. Don't worry! He'll draw them!'

'Capital!' said Bowyer. 'You're a good partner, Phayre, and in a few days our patience will be rewarded.'

They went out of the office together, and, when Phayre had opened the door, Bowyer went quickly down the dark side of the street toward the station. Phayre stood looking after him.

'I'd give a good deal to know just how much you know about Joe Bostock's death,' he mused.

20

The Conflagration

'I'm going back to work for you, Mr. Phayre,' Wilton had said when he left the office. And he had meant it. Without any further hope of keeping the line for Kitty, he resolved, for the work's sake, that the day when the control passed into Bowyer's hands should see the grade across Big Muskeg.

He found the camp in much the same condition as when he had left it. Andersen reported that the men were still getting liquor, and were slacking. Wilton, whose mind had no room for rival propositions at the same time, dismissed the subject. That would be settled next; for the present he wanted a long sleep in which to shake off his depression, and with which to nerve himself for his task.

He went straight to bed. But he was

aroused by Andersen a little after midnight.

'There's a big blaze a couple of miles north of us,' said the foreman. 'Sprung up like lightning. And a gale's sweeping up the swamp. The men won't turn out to backfire. They say it's Saturday night — and most of them are drunk.'

Wilton put on his clothes quickly, placed Jules in charge of the shack and hurried to the bunkhouses. Already the air was thick with haze. There had been no rain for two weeks, and a succession of heavy frosts had killed the ferns and undergrowth, leaving them as dry as tinder. It was dangerous weather.

The workmen obeyed Wilton's summons with slow sullenness. They were stupid with drink, and it was clear that they had no intention of being robbed of their traditional Sunday morning sleep. They showed an ugly disposition toward him. Some jeered; some refused to turn out at all. But some of the engineers and foremen were already hurrying to the scene. Wilton collected these and started with them in the direction of the conflagration.

This was soon seen to be serious. Under the high wind the fire was speeding down at a terrific rate toward the camp, filling the air with dense clouds of smoke. The camp, having cleared ways on three sides, had not been fire-guarded. These should have been wide enough to protect it under ordinary circumstances, and the work that was being pushed had left no time for anything else. But from the swift rate at which the fire was seen to be advancing it was dubious whether the cleared ways would hold it.

Back-firing was impossible, for the wind came up the cleared road from the muskeg with hurricane force. Wilton posted his men along the near side of the way, to beat out the patches of flame that would spring up from the burning brands carried over it by the wind.

The fire was fiercest along the muskeg edge, where, fanned by the full force of the gale, it was sweeping down upon the camp. Wilton took up his station here, with a half-dozen of his assistants, armed with branches.

They had not long to wait, for the

conflagration came roaring down on them before many minutes had passed. It seemed to gather force as it advanced. The smoke was stifling, and the air filled with burning embers of boughs, that sailed high overhead and dropped into the branches of the trees behind them. They could see one another only dimly in the swirling fog.

The line of fire shot through the crackling ferns and undergrowth before them, and reached the edge of the cleared way. Tongues of flame leaped up at them in furious derision, patches of grass began to smoulder along the track. The men worked madly. For a few moments the clearing seemed to have stayed the progress of the devouring element.

Then the workers found themselves surrounded with a ring of flame. The trees and grass were alight behind them. And along the muskeg edge the conflagration had thrust out gripping tentacles of flame that edged round and in toward the engine-sheds.

Shouting to those nearest him to follow, Wilton ran down toward the swamp. But when the grade came into sight he saw something that caught his cry and killed it on his lips. Of a sudden his veins seemed to run ice for blood. The fire had caught the trestling and was running along the timbers, eating its way toward the east bank. The trestle was a fiery thread across the black level of the muskeg.

But what made him catch his breath and clench his fists was this: the fire was moving eastward, and yet it could not have started on the west bank, for here the trestling was completely hidden under the foundation, over which the flames could not pass. The fire had started in the middle of the muskeg, and had been started there of design.

It was the end of everything. Big Muskeg would remain un-spanned after all, when Bowyer assumed control.

Wilton ran back. The smoke was whirling all along the cleared way, and there was a wall of fire on either side of it. He plunged through in the direction of the camp. He saw the figures of the fire-fighters, battling in a score of places as fire after fire leaped up, apparently out of cleared ground, and roared skyward.

He caught two men as they reeled past him. 'The horses!' he shouted.

They ran toward the stables. Brands had set the timbers ablaze in several places. Inside the horses whinnied and shrieked, plunging and struggling in their stalls.

They broke down the door, and had just time to dodge the maddened herd that sprang for the entrance. There was a furious melee of hoofs and tearing teeth, and the animals broke frantically toward the muskeg.

Little could be seen in the smoke, and less could be done now. Everywhere were pillars of flame from burning buildings. The men's quarters in the heart of the open ground seemed safe, but the long sheds of supplies, containing miles of rails, were blazing furiously, sending up great banners of fire, tipped with brushes of smoke that spread fanwise high overhead across muskeg and forest.

The engine-houses were fire-red ruins, belching up a black, sticky smoke that clogged the fighters' lungs and settled in fine particles of black dust all over them. Drums of oil and gasoline exploded with the salvoes of artillery, shooting up streamers of flame sky-high. Rivulets of fire broke forth and streamed through the camp, spreading the destruction.

The encircling arms of the conflagration had thrust their fingers all about them through the forest, which was ablaze in every direction. But in the open space itself the fire had been stayed, though hardly anything was left except the kitchens and bunkhouses. The sheds and engine-houses had gone up in a few minutes, and now glowed fiercely with an intense heat, but without flame.

The fighters had done all they could do, and that was nothing. They could do nothing more now, except to guard the bunkhouses from the rivers of blazing oil. Wilton found a few men and told them to take spades and throw up mounds along the courses of these torrents, in order to divert them.

Nearer the muskeg the great sheds blazed from end to end, making the night bright as day, and illuminating the whole country for miles around. It was impossible to approach within a hundred yards of them.

The laborers, mad with drink, gathered in clusters at the doors of the bunkhouses and jeered at the men who had fought to save them; and these, too disconsolate to care, having at last secured the remaining structures, flung down their spades and drew out of their way. Everyone knew this was the end. Three men came arm in arm toward Wilton out of the smoke, shouting and hiccoughing. He stood aside and let them stagger past him. It did not matter. Out of the smoke came the figure of McGee, the head locomotive engineer. His hair was crisped, his face blackened, and the tears had furrowed white channels down his cheeks.

'It's all gone!' he shouted. 'Nothing but scrap-iron and junk. We'll have a bargain-sale!' He recognized Wilton and seized him by the arm. 'Who set that blaze?' he screamed. 'Man, there was gasoline, gallons of it, soaking the sheds before ever the fire come there. They were soaked with it. Who did it? Show me the damn skunk!' he shouted, half beside himself.

'It doesn't matter now,' said Wilton.

McGee raved, cursing and sobbing, and suddenly rushed away into the smoke and was lost to view. Two or three of the fire-fighters stumbled past. They were dog-tired, and walked with bowed heads and bent knees. Their clothing hung about them in charred fragments.

Wilton was making his way toward his shack before it occurred to him that he would not find it. Yet there was the safe. He would stay guard over that. To his immense surprise, however, he discovered that the shack had escaped the conflagration, though nothing remained of Kitty's but a few blackened beams. A back-fire had been set successfully. The grass was burned all about the place, and some of the timbers were scorched, but that was all. The shack was an oasis in the devastation of cinders. Jules had stuck to his post.

Wilton knew there had been treachery. He knew that Bowyer's appearance at the portage had not been chance. Bowyer had not driven miles from Cold Junction by coincidence. Wilton had no doubt that the fire was of his making.

And even that did not matter.

At the door of his shack he stopped. He had a strange instinct of danger — the instinct of the beast returning to its den, which tells it that something has been there during its absence. The lamp that he had left upon the table was burning still, and nothing seemed to have altered; and yet the sense of danger came to Wilton and grew.

He unlocked the office door and went in. For a moment he thought his suspicions groundless. Then he saw that the door of the safe was open. He ran to it, and found the papers inside and apparently intact, just as they had been.

Jules must have scared the thieves away before they could accomplish their design. But how had they got the combination?

Doubtless the fire, set on the chance of burning out the camp, had also been designed to draw him and all the men in charge away, while the attempt was made.

Wilton shouted for Jules, and then,

remembering that the deaf-mute could not hear him, went out of the room toward the little wooden outbuilding which Jules had constructed for his abode. But the Muskegon was not there.

He went back through the kitchen. In the middle of the room he saw something dimly outlined on the floor. He struck a match and found Jules in a pool of blood. One side of his head had been almost battered to pieces with a hatchet that lay on the floor nearby.

And yet Jules was not dead, for, as Wilton bent over him, he opened his eyes and smiled very faintly into his master's face. And the fingers of one outstretched hand quivered and pointed toward the office.

Wilton raised Jules gently in his arms and carried him within, and laid him on the floor. The Indian was almost at his last gasp, and he seemed struggling to express something before he died.

The fluttering fingers pointed upward. All that was left of life within the broken body seemed to be concentrated in them. Wilton watched them; he had no idea what Jules wanted, but, if he was expressing a wish, he was resolved that it should be gratified, and that the Indian should die contented.

The fingers squirmed and twisted. It seemed to Wilton that there was something in the room that Jules wanted. They were pointing now toward the safe. Wilton raised the dying man in his arms and supported the shoulders against his knees, so that Jules might see.

Jules pointed straight at the safe, looked up, and nodded. Wilton nodded. Jules seemed to lose interest then, but the fingers still twisted, and now they pointed toward the wall behind. Wilton shifted his position, and raised the shade of the lamp, to illuminate the other half of the room.

The fingers wandered over the woodwork, and stopped upon the caricature of Lee Chambers that Jules had drawn. Jules Halfhead smiled up into Wilton's face and nodded. Wilton nodded. Then Jules died.

21

Kidnapped!

Since Bowyer's last visit to the store, Molly had been making plans; but when these were complete, she did not dare to place them before the factor.

She knew that they could not long remain at the portage. There was his increasing infirmity; there was Tom Bowyer's enmity — his hold over her father, which was bringing him into his grave.

Yet she feared one of the factor's wild outbursts of rage if she renewed her suggestion that they should go to Winnipeg. On the other hand, gradually she began to believe that McDonald was forming plans of his own. If that were so, in due time, and in his own way, he would talk to her about them.

Meanwhile nothing had happened. The muskeg seemed like a knife-thrust into her heart, for beyond that was all her world, from which she was forever banned.

She watched her father anxiously. He still dragged his leg as he walked, and the fear that was always upon him now had made him an old man within the past year. The girl's love for him, which her humiliation at Bowyer's hands had never entirely killed, burned up again after she had broken with Wilton.

But she wondered constantly about the power that Bowyer had over her father. Had McDonald given her any encouragement she would have spoken to him, and begged for an understanding that might remove the cloud which hung over them both. But the factor was more morose than ever, especially when the winter trading ended, and time hung heavily upon their hands.

'Ye'll no see Will Carruthers again, lass?' McDonald had asked her once.

She shook her head. 'And Mr. Bowyer?' asked the old man hopefully.

'I never want to see him again,' she answered.

The factor's face grew purple, and he seemed on the verge of one of his frenzied outbreaks. But suddenly the gray shadow of his fear came on his face. He flung his hands up, as if fearing a blow, and turned and went up to his room, dragging his leg behind him.

The talk came at last. McDonald was in his chair upstairs, Molly reading to him. But the factor did not seem to hear her; he was looking out of the window and brooding as of old. Suddenly he turned to her.

'I'm thinking of leaving here before winter, lass,' he said.

'Leaving here, Father? For good?'

'For aye,' he exploded. 'I thocht I'd die here and be laid beside your mother. And I've held on! God, how I've held on! But I'm done with that hope. Would ye leave the portage, Molly?' he asked wistfully.

'Yes, Father! I wish we could. I wish we could go somewhere together where we'd never have cause to remember it.'

'Aye, never to remember it!' he echoed.

'To Winnipeg?' she suggested timidly.

He seemed to tremble at her words. He turned fiercely upon her. 'To Scotland!'

he shouted. 'I'm done with this country. A man's thochts turn in his old age to his homeland. To Aberdeen!'

She leaned her head against his shoulder. 'I'll go with you to Aberdeen, Father,' she said. 'I believe you will be happy there and grow well again. But it'll cost money — '

'I have the money, Molly. I havena worked for nought all these years. Twelve thousand in the bank at Yorkton. It'll take us hame and keep us.'

Molly was awed by the old man's fanatical enthusiasm. 'When shall we go?' she asked.

'This autumn, lass — before the snows fall. But — ' He clutched her by the arm. ' — ye'll say nought about it?'

'But you must arrange with the Company for a new factor, and, if he isn't trained — '

His clutch became convulsive. 'Not a word!' he cried fiercely. 'Havena I done weel by the Company? It won't be the sufferer. If they thocht I was going away they'd — not a word, lass! Promise me!'

'But the Indians will come to trade — '

'I tell ye we darena let them know!' he whimpered. 'Molly, lass, ye winna go back on me now?'

'No, I won't go back on you,' she answered.

But she did not like the idea of stealing away, although the Company would suffer little. And then there would be the forfeiture of his pension. But she dared not bring up that subject in view of his evident obsession.

Thereafter, though he said nothing more, Molly knew that he was making mental preparations for the journey. He dragged himself about the store and the portage, as if taking his last farewell of the inanimate objects that had grown to be a part of his life. And once, missing him, she found him by the grave under the tamaracks, kneeling as if in prayer, with the tears raining down his furrowed cheeks.

After a while, they began to make preparations. They spoke of the journey as being weeks, instead of months, away. Then came a night when the factor tapped at Molly's door. She dressed quickly and went out of her room, to see the whole skyline ablaze. Clouds of smoke were whirling down on them. Suddenly a rig with two horses came dashing across the portage and drew up at the door.

Molly recognized Lee Chambers and Hackett, and turned and faced them, though her heart was beating with fear. They leaped out and ran up to her.

'We've come for you, Miss McDonald,' shouted Lee Chambers. 'The fire's across the muskeg, and there won't be anything left of this store in twenty minutes. Come along!'

He shouted and gesticulated wildly, and seemed hardly master of himself. McDonald started and looked out through the smoke clouds. But as they approached the girl she drew herself away.

'It's not true!' she cried. 'The fire's on the other side. Why should you come for us?'

'I tell you you'll be burned to a cinder inside of fifteen minutes!' yelled Chambers. 'We've got no time to waste. We're going to drive you out of danger. Come along!'

'I won't come!' cried Molly. 'Don't go with them, Father. He's not speaking the truth! Look at his face!'

Hackett pushed Chambers out of his way and strode up to the door. 'I guess that's true enough, what you said, Miss McDonald,' he said. 'The fire ain't this side — but Will Carruthers is dying. They pulled him out of his shack. He's in a bad way. Mebbe he'll just live till morning. He's calling for you!'

'Will — Will burned!' gasped Molly, looking at him with eyes of horror.

'It's gospel truth!' cried Chambers. 'He can't rest till you go to him.'

'Then why did you tell us that lie?' asked the girl, searching his face as if to read to the bottom of his soul.

'Because we wanted to break it gently,' shouted Hackett. He seized her by the arm. 'We haven't no time to waste!' he shouted. 'He may die any minute while we're talking here.'

'He didn't send you,' cried Molly with sudden conviction. 'Why should he have sent *you*? We won't go. You're *lying!* Let me go!'

She pushed her father back into the store and tried to bolt the door in their faces, but they set their shoulders against it and broke through. Molly ran to her room; they were there almost as soon as she. She screamed. She heard McDonald's feeble shout cut off as Chambers grasped him by the throat. And then she was struggling madly in Hackett's arms.

'Curse you!' he shouted, with a string of vile oaths, seizing her by the hair and dashing his fist into her face.

She fought back like a tigress, broke from him, and, snatching up the water-pitcher, smashed it across his head, cutting his face with the fragments of porcelain. He grasped her by the throat. She clung to the bed, the table, to the door, screaming the while until his fingers tightened on her throat and the room swam blackly around her.

She was faintly conscious of a gag thrust into her mouth, of being carried, struggling, out of the store, of being lifted into the rig. Then she revived to find herself huddled upon the floor, her father bending over her with his wrists tied, and mumbling in her ear. The engineer, seated in front of them, was driving furiously along the trail southward. Hackett, with one leg thrust out on either side of the vehicle, was wiping the blood from his face.

He saw that Molly was conscious, and bent and pulled the gag out of her mouth.

'I guess that'll hold you, my beauty!' he jeered. 'I caught a wildcat once, but it hadn't nothing on you! If you move I'll bash your face in!'

Desperate as she was, Molly would have tried to leap from the rig but for her father. She heard him continue mumbling; and at length the meaning of his words reached her brain, and the horror of them numbed her and repressed all thought of fighting.

'It'll be all right, my lass,' the old man was muttering. 'They won't hurt you no more. They're taking us to Tom Bowyer, I reckon. He's bested us. We'll have to give in. We'll make the most of it.'

The old man shook with fear, but he laid his hand caressingly upon her head. And afterward Molly recalled that gesture, and remembered that it was his right one.

At the time she thought nothing. She lay back with her head against the seat, resolved to husband her strength for a more desperate struggle later, if need be. Her dress was rent, her hair fell to her waist. Hackett grinned at her in frank admiration.

'If you'll be real good I'll let you sit on the seat beside me,' he said, leering.

Molly shuddered. But a sudden lurch of the rig, in a deep rut checked his approaches. He swore fiercely at Chambers, who swore back in a high, whinnying cry. Rain had begun to fall; the horses, lashed incessantly, tore madly through the darkness, and the rig swayed dangerously from side to side.

Molly's thoughts ran on as fiercely. They were taking her to Bowyer, then! But Bowyer was at Cold Junction, and surely he could not harm her there! And he was taking her father. She must remain at his side and protect him. She sat passively upon the floor, hearing the frenzied babbling of the old man, and soothing him with one hand stretched out upon his.

But this was not the way to Cold

Junction! The vehicle had turned into a stony upland, with a few patches of thin forest scattered here and there. This desolate region led toward Chain of Lakes, where several fishing clubs had purchased ground and water rights and set up camps. Her heart sank. She caught at Hackett's arm.

'Where are you taking us?' she pleaded. 'Won't you let us go back? I'll say nothing if you let us go — I'll say nothing!'

Hackett grinned at her and tried to put his arm about her. She struck out at him, and, with an oath, he pushed her back violently into the bottom of the rig.

She gathered all her courage to wait. And the waiting was not long. The upland was surmounted, and a lake came into sight, a neck of land, and the dark outlines of camp buildings upon it. A light showed in a window. Chambers pulled up the horses.

He leaped to the ground and, catching McDonald by the arm, pulled him roughly out of the vehicle. He hammered fiercely upon the door, which opened. Tom Bowyer appeared on the threshold.

The factor began to tremble. Bowyer pulled him unceremoniously inside.

'Bring her in!' he yelled to Hackett.

The outlaw caught Molly by the waist and swung her to the ground. She tried to break from him, but Bowyer, having thrust McDonald inside, snatched her from Hackett's grasp and, picking her up bodily, carried her into the lighted room.

It was the club-room. Hunting trophies were on the walls — horns of moose and caribou. There was a table, a divan, and a number of chairs. A partition of pine planks divided it from a room behind it. Curtains hung before the windows.

Bowyer deposited the girl on the divan, went out, and pushed McDonald in after her. Outside Molly heard a fierce altercation in progress — Bowyer's threatening tones, Hackett's sullen answers, and Lee Chambers' querulous whine.

Presently the two men went out, and Molly heard the horses being led away. She tried to adjust her torn dress, to fasten up her hair. Bowyer came back.

'*Now* we'll have a few words together,' he said, leering at Molly.

22

Tonguay Talks

Wilton carried the dead man into his room and laid the body on the bed. His face was set like flint. In this he traced the work of Bowyer; but the tool, Lee Chambers, was the object of his immediate vengeance.

Before anything else, he must discover the motive of the burglary.

He opened the safe, which he had shut, and went through the papers very deliberately. He imagined that he would be able to discover immediately what had been abstracted. He was astonished to find that everything appeared intact, and just as he had left it.

The object of the burglary should have been the bundle of engineering records, from which the secret of the location of the new wheat lands might have been ascertained. There were also the blue-prints showing the proposed ranges and townships, which would have afforded a ready clue. But these had not even been disturbed.

Wilton could not understand it! He tried to figure it out. He had already come to the conclusion that the fire had been started with the purpose of drawing himself and those in the vicinity away from the office, while the burglary was being committed. But why had it failed? And what had Chambers been after?

He might have taken flight in terror after committing the murder, without prosecuting his search. Or, again, he might have been after money.

But Chambers must have known that there was no money in the safe. The men's pay came up monthly by special messenger, and was handed out the same evening. It would arrive on the Monday. Chambers could not have been after spoil of that kind.

Wilton looked through Joe's papers again. Everything seemed intact, and nothing had even been tampered with. It must have been that Chambers took fright after the murder.

He closed the safe again. Outside the smoke was clearing. The fire had passed the limits of the camp, leaving a wilderness of charred tree trunks, still glowing red and lurid in the moonlight. Only the long sheds still burned fiercely down by the muskeg. But the noise from the bunkhouses was increasing. Wild yells, drunken oaths, outbursts of cheering came to Wilton's ears.

Suddenly Andersen came running across the smoking ground, followed by some half-dozen of the engineers. The foreman came panting up to the door of the shack.

'The men are crazy drunk, Mr. Carruthers, and they're planning to attack the office!' he gasped.

'What do they think they'll get here?' demanded Wilton.

'Somebody's been telling them the safe's full of money, and that they're going to be laid off because of the fire.'

'That last part's true enough,' said Wilton. 'The first isn't. You've seen those liquor sellers?' he demanded sharply.

The foreman nodded. 'They was in

camp tonight during the fire,' he said. 'I didn't see the use of telling you then.'

Wilton reflected a moment, while the engineers gathered anxiously about him. With coal-black faces, and in their cinders of clothes, they looked like devils rather than men.

'They can't open the safe,' said Wilton. 'At least, there's only one man can, and he's been at it already. No, never mind what I mean! I don't want bloodshed. I'll open it and show it to them.' He turned to one of the engineers. 'Take four men with you and hurry to the store, and see that no harm comes to Miss McDonald and her father,' he ordered. 'And take this,' he added, picking the revolver out of the drawer and handing it to him.

'You'd better come, too, Mr. Carruthers,' the man suggested.

'No, I'll stay here,' said Wilton. 'Hurry!'

The engineer picked four men, and they hurried down the road. Andersen and two others remained with Wilton. Hardly had the party left when the mob came streaming out of the bunkhouses toward the office, shouting and yelling.

They carried crowbars and long-handled axes, and were evidently mad with drink.

Seeing the four men standing in the doorway, however, they hesitated to rush them, probably in the belief that they were armed, and stood off, cursing them.

'Speak up!' shouted Wilton. 'What is it you men want?'

The shouts died away to a muttering. A spokesman stepped forward.

'We want the money in the safe, and we'll have it,' he shouted. 'We all know you set the fire because the line's busted, and you've got the safe chock full of money. You've worked us like dogs all summer, and now you're going to lay us off because the Company's busted. You'd better hand it over.'

Evidently somebody had been telling the men that tale. Wilton was anxious to try peaceful methods.

'There's no money in the safe,' he answered. 'Send a deputation of three men, and you can examine it.'

The laborers, who for the most part understood him very well, looked at one another uncertainly. They were as docile as lambs without leadership. But they had a leader; the outlaw Tonguay stepped forward out of the crowd.

'Come along, boys, he's fooling you!' he yelled. 'Smash his head for him! Give them what's coming to them!'

But he slunk back into their midst as the bellowing mob rushed forward. Wilton noticed that he was fingering a revolver in his coat pocket. He waited till the mob was close upon the shack. He had calculated that an instant's hesitation would follow, seized it, and sprang into their midst, striking out right and left, and felling a drunken laborer with every blow. As Tonguay fumbled desperately with the trigger of the weapon in his pocket, Wilton dealt him a smashing blow that knocked him senseless. He stopped, took the revolver, and turned and faced his assailants.

'Now, men,' he said crisply, 'I've told you that you shall examine the safe, and I'll keep my word. Three of you can enter. The rest will wait outside.'

After a pause three of the workmen came forward uncertainly. Wilton took them inside the shack, opened the safe door, and took out the contents, package by package.

'Satisfied there's no money?' he asked.

'I guess that's so,' admitted the leader of the men reluctantly.

'Then get out,' said Wilton, driving them toward the door.

The three rejoined their companions, and, with sullen mutterings, the workmen lurched away aimlessly, and totally unable to unite on any further plan of aggression, now that their leader was gone. Andersen and one of the engineers picked up Tonguay and brought him into the shack. The man was still unconscious. Wilton's blow had struck him fairly on the point of the jaw, paralyzing the plexus of facial nerves. However, he showed signs of coming to shortly.

'Jules is dead,' said Wilton quietly.

'Jules dead?' shouted Andersen.

'Murdered. It was Lee Chambers. He must have been hanging round the camp. He got into the safe, too, but was scared away before he took anything. Come inside!'

At the sight of the dead man on the bed Andersen swore softly. There were hard looks on the faces of all. They liked Wilton and knew of the troubles of the line; that had not been their business, but the homicide stirred them to the depths.

'The horses are on the edge of the swamp, Mr. Carruthers,' said one of the engineers, a Scotchman named McLaren. 'We can catch and saddle them and scour the country. It's my belief he wasn't alone.'

'He wasn't,' said Wilton.

'He must have been with those two liquor peddlers,' said Andersen. 'I guess they set the fire, all right.'

'I guess they did,' said Wilton. 'And I want to go on to the next camp and telephone in to Clayton, and get the police up here right away.'

'I done it, Mr. Carruthers,' said Andersen. 'You see, sir, just as soon as the fire begun I seen that gasoline on the engine-sheds. And I'd heard the men talking, because I picked up a little of their language. I knew there was trouble coming, and I 'phoned Mr. Quain. He said he'd get an engine and come right up with some of his men.'

'Well done!' said Wilton. 'We'll have this man for them, at any rate.'

Tonguay stirred, muttered, and suddenly sat up on the floor, looking at his captors in bewilderment. He put his hand to his head and groaned. Wilton quietly took the revolver out of his pocket and walked toward him.

'I'm going to ask you a few questions, Tonguay,' he remarked in a casual tone. 'You'll find it to your advantage to answer them. Who sent you here?'

At the sound of his name Tonguay shrank back and shot a sullen glance at Wilton.

'Who sent you here tonight?' repeated Wilton. 'Was it the same man who sent you to arrest me last December?'

Tonguay broke into a short laugh. 'You t'ink dey tell that to me?' he sneered. 'Jim Hackett don't tell me not'ings. He say you got de job — you do it!'

'You came with Hackett; but what was the game? You were told to sell liquor round the camp and make the workmen drunk and discontented. I guess you have an idea whom you were working for, besides Jim Hackett, eh, Tonguay?'

'Mebbe I do,' muttered the outlaw. 'I guess you shoot me unless I say Mr. Bowyer, eh?'

The parry was effective. 'You came here with Hackett and Lee Chambers to fire the camp,' said Wilton. 'Lee Chambers' job was to steal papers from the safe while we were fighting the fire. You were going to meet somewhere afterward. Where was it?'

Tonguay was silent.

'You'll answer,' said Wilton, raising the revolver.

The man burst into scornful laughter. 'You don't bluff me,' he jeered. 'I guess you don' want to be charged wit' anodder murder, eh?'

'Do you?' asked Wilton.

'How's dat? You don' fix no murder on me.'

'Come here!' said Wilton, taking him by the arm and leading him to the door of the bedroom.

The moon, sloping in the west, threw a

flood of light on the white face of Jules, showing the crushed skull and the blood-clots that stained the pillow. Tonguay screamed and started away, but Wilton held him fast.

'Lee Chambers' work. A hanging job, my friend,' he said grimly. 'You'd better answer me now, if you want a chance of getting out of this with a straight neck.'

'What you want to know?' babbled the outlaw.

'Where were you three going to meet afterward?'

'In de club-house of de fishing-camp at Chain of Lakes, twelve miles south,' groaned Tonguay, sinking back against the wall.

The four men exchanged glances. The fishing season was ended, the shooting season, owing to an act of the legislature, would not open for two weeks more. It was an ideal place for hiding.

'That's where we'll find them,' said Andersen.

Wilton handed him the revolver. 'You'll guard your prisoner, and hand him over to the police when they arrive,' he said.

Then he saw men running toward the shack, and stepped outside. It was the party whom he had sent to the portage.

'They're gone!' panted one of them.

'Gone? What do you mean?' shouted Wilton.

'Miss McDonald and the factor. They went to bed last night. Now — they're not there. There's been foul work done, and a fight. Her room is all in confusion, the bed-clothes dragged into the store, a pitcher smashed to pieces.'

Andersen pulled at Wilton's sleeve. 'We'll catch the horses at the muskeg,' he said. 'You stay here. It's our job, sir.'

'No, it's my job, Andersen,' answered Wilton; 'and, by God, it'll be a thorough one!'

23

Wilton Rides Alone

He ran down toward the swamp, followed by the party of engineers. The horses, having recovered from their fright, were grazing along the edge; they were wary, however, and would not let themselves be approached. For some minutes the men made fruitless efforts to surround them.

However, the animals soon got mired in the muskeg, which impeded their movements without actually holding them, and the men, being lighter, were able to run across the surface. Soon a cordon was formed, and Wilton managed to catch the mane of a big draught-beast which had been in the front row of the grading-yokes, and, despite its clumsy appearance, had taken the saddle and had a tolerable action.

But hardly had he made sure of it by a grasp on the mane and upper lip than the remainder, snorting and flourishing their heels, dashed through the cordon and galloped full speed toward the lake.

'We'll be with you in a minute, Mr. Carruthers!' shouted one of the men as they went in pursuit.

But Wilton, without answering, had sprung on the beast's back, and, leaning forward, caught the broken halter and guided it across the swamp. There were saddles in the factor's store, and, much as he grudged the time, he decided to saddle and bridle the animal.

He had no doubt that the outlaws who had set the fire were responsible for Molly's abduction, and, if the trail led up to Bowyer, as he was sure it would, God help Bowyer!

In a couple of minutes he had put on the saddle and tautened the girth, bridled the animal, and was riding hard along the southward trail, unarmed.

Meanwhile, the rest of the party spent a fruitless half-hour trying to catch horses. At length, after a consultation, they hurried back to the camp, collected a few more Canadians and Americans, and started out after Wilton, leaving a half-dozen to keep the workmen in check. But the laborers, exhausted after their debauch were, for the most part, asleep; only a few rolled hiccoughing about the exterior of the bunkhouses, indulging in aimless demonstrations against the shack, which the presence of the volunteer guard promptly checked.

In the shack Tonguay stared apathetically at Andersen, who sat with the revolver in his hand, keeping watch over his captive.

'You t'ink I kill dat feller, eh?' he demanded after a while.

'I dunno, my friend,' answered Andersen. 'If you did, I guess you'll swing for it, all right.'

'See here! Jim Hackett tole me to come here an' tell de men dere's money in de safe, an' dey're fools to be worked like dogs and den be laid off because de company's busted. Dat's all I know. I tole dem to get der pay what was coming to dem.'

'Posseebly,' said Andersen. 'You was a fool to do it, though. That story's for the police; it ain't for me. You can tell the inspector when he gets here.'

Tonguay leaped from the chair on which he sat. 'What's dat?' he screamed. 'De police come here, you tell me?'

'Sure, they're coming! What did you think?'

'See here! You let me go!' yelled Tonguay. 'I didn't do not'ing. What for you arrest me?'

'Boss's orders,' said Andersen gruffly. 'That'll be enough. Set down like a good feller, now.'

Tonguay made a flying leap for the door. Andersen, interposing, put out his leg, and the outlaw sprawled his length upon the floor. He looked up into the muzzle of the revolver.

'If you try that again you'll get a taste of what you give Jules there,' said Andersen.

'You lie! I tell you I didn't do dat!' screamed Tonguay, sinking back into his chair and shuddering.

They watched each other for some time. It was beginning to grow light. Suddenly the trample of horses was heard outside. Then Inspector Quain appeared at the door of the shack, accompanied by four mounted constables. They were in full kit, with bandoliers slung across their shoulders, and carried their short-barreled Rosses.

The men on guard came running up with the news of the outrage at the store. Quain listened, nodded. 'Had considerable trouble, eh?' he said, dismounting and casting a glance about him at the burned-out buildings and the still burning sheds.

'That fire was set by enemies of the Missatibi,' shouted one of the engineers. 'And we've got one of the men in there!' He pointed toward the shack.

Quain went in. 'Who's this man you've got here?' he asked Andersen.

'I dunno,' said the Swede, 'except that he's been making trouble in the camp, and he led the crowd tonight. They wanted to bust the safe open.'

Quain turned to his men, who were awaiting the order to dismount. 'Round up those men in their bunkhouses and keep the lot of 'em under guard!' he said, pointing toward the groups of laborers that had gathered about the horses.

The constables drove the laborers back toward their quarters. 'Two of you'll be enough!' shouted Quain after them. 'The other two — Beckett and James — will dismount and rest their horses. I'll want you chaps!'

'You've had some trouble,' said Quain to Andersen.

'Why, this ain't trouble, inspector,' answered the Swede. 'You yust look inside that room. I guess it ain't the worst, what I told you already.'

Quain strode to the door of Wilton's bedroom, uttered a sharp exclamation, and bent over the body of Jules. He came back quickly.

'Who killed that Indian?' he asked.

'Lee Chambers, I guess.'

'Tell me what you know. Look sharp, please!'

'Why, all I know is he done some crooked work on the trestling and beat it out of camp before Mr. Carruthers had time to fire him. Then Mr. Carruthers caught him prowling round the safe one night. Last night he come back after the fire, which I guess that feller there knows something about.'

'I tell you I don' know not'ing!' yelled

Tonguay, who seemed in the extremity of panic.

'Mr. Carruthers said Mr. Chambers killed Jules there and got into the safe. I dunno no more than that. But — '

Suddenly, with a frenzied scream, Tonguay leaped from his chair and darted for the door again. Andersen was just quick enough. He caught him on the door-sill, and the two men struggled furiously. Tonguay snatched Andersen's revolver out of his hand. Andersen's hand closed on the outlaw's wrist.

Quain ran to grasp Tonguay's arm, but, before he could hold it, the struggle ended. For Tonguay had got his finger on the trigger and was trying to bring the weapon in line with Andersen's head. Andersen swung the outlaw's arm around, and the bullet, discharged too late, passed through Tonguay's left arm.

Screaming with pain and fear, the man rolled on the floor, and surrendered himself passively to the ministrations of the inspector and Andersen.

The spectators, who had gathered outside the shack, had come running in at the sound of the shot. Quain ordered them out, and, taking off Tonguay's coat, he cut the sleeve of his shirt away. One of the constables brought him his first-aid case, and he soon had the wound painted with iodine and bandaged.

'I'll put a blanket on the floor for the poor feller,' said Andersen, as Tonguay collapsed in a dead faint in the chair where they had placed him.

'I'll not need you any further,' said the inspector. 'You'll help keep the men in their bunkhouses, in case of trouble. Take three or four of your own men. I'm going after Carruthers, and I expect to be back by noon.'

He called one of the two men whom he had dismounted.

'You'll be on duty here until relieved,' he said. 'You will take charge of this man. Also that safe!' He pointed toward it. 'Remember that under no circumstances is anyone to be permitted to enter.'

The man saluted him. Quain called the second dismounted constable, and they rode off at a swift pace toward the portage.

24

Bowyer's Hour

As Bowyer came back into the room Molly ran to her father, as if to shield him. The very presence of the man seemed to throw the old factor into the extremity of terror. He was trembling from head to foot, and looked utterly helpless and pathetic as he cowered before his persecutor.

Bowyer looked the incarnation of insolence and triumph as he stood in the doorway, red-faced, red-haired, like some sleek fox that has put off its habitual cunning because it is at last secure from danger.

His vicious eyes fixed themselves upon the girl's face as she fastened back the hair that hung about her. He stood before her, mocking, and yet with an undercurrent of determination that the girl sensed, and knew she would require all her wits to combat.

'That brute was rough with you,' said

Bowyer. 'But I guess you gave him better than he gave you. I guess he got what he deserved. I told them you weren't to come to any harm. Well, McDonald, they didn't use you too rough, eh?'

'We were brought here by force and violence,' said Molly defiantly. 'Are we to be kept here in the same way?'

'You are, my dear,' jeered Bowyer. 'You've got a little lesson to learn about law in this country. You were going to have me whipped, eh?'

'And I would still, and will!' she flamed out. 'Let us go immediately!'

'By George, you're splendid when you look like that!' said Bowyer, breathing thickly. Molly realized her mistake; her anger only added fuel to his passion. She tried to compose herself.

Suddenly he stepped forward and took her hands in his. 'Molly — listen to me now,' he said. 'Listen quietly. I'm not going to hurt you. I did what I did because I wanted you. I love you. I've got to have you, Molly. But I want you to love me. Let's forget it all. What'd you say, Molly? Did you ever think of what I've got to offer you?'

She tried to draw her hands away, but he held them tightly, and, remembering her resolution, she stood with them passive in his own.

'What's your answer, Molly?' asked Bowyer.

'*Never!*' she cried. 'You knew that! Did you think I was going to change because you had had me kidnapped and inflicted this outrage upon me?'

Bowyer turned toward the factor. 'Maybe she'll obey you, McDonald,' he said softly; and something in his tone arrested the girl's attention.

Bowyer was threatening, not pleading, and McDonald was gray with fear. He leaped up. 'Molly, he means it!' he screamed. 'We can't escape him. He'll get you as he's got me. Molly, say 'yes' to him, because he's won. He'll get what he wants, anyway. And it's no shame to see when you're beaten, and to give way.'

The sight of the trembling old man swept away all the girl's resolve. Her loathing for their persecutor drove her to frenzy. She tore her hands from Bowyer's, ran behind the divan, and snatched up a rifle that stood there. She raised the stock above her head with both hands.

'If you touch me again, I'll kill you!' she cried.

Bowyer looked at the factor. 'Then I'll tell her what I know,' he said. 'For years I've stood by you and shielded you — '

The factor's hands went up as if he were warding off a blow, and there was the mute appeal of a whipped dog in his eyes. Bowyer went on: 'For years I've protected you from the law. Now I've done with you.'

'You can tell *me*, Tom Bowyer!' cried Molly.

He swung toward her. '*I'll* tell you, *then*,' he roared. 'Your father's a *murderer*. He's been wanted by the police these twenty years and more, and he's still wanted. *The police don't forget.* I knew it from the first. He came to me and asked my help after he'd murdered a man in a common brawl. He wanted to give himself up. I told him not to. I got him his job at the portage, where he'd be secure. I've stood by him, been his friend, protected him. But I'll protect him no more.'

He wheeled upon the factor. 'Now speak to her *again!*' he shouted. 'You're her father!' There was intense mockery in his tone. 'She'll *obey* you. Ask her if she wants you to swing in the jail-yard at Yorkton while she's on her honeymoon with Will Carruthers!'

His brutality seemed to strike down the last spark of McDonald's manhood. With a whimpering cry the factor dropped to his knees and hid his face in his hands. Molly let the rifle fall and shrank back against the wall. A cry broke from her lips.

'It isn't true, Father!' she begged, fixing her eyes in terror upon the factor's. 'Tell him it isn't true. You didn't kill that man who insulted my mother! And, if you did, you did it to protect her. Tell him it's a lie!'

The factor's whimpering moans were all her answer. They ceased, and for a full minute there was not the least sound in the room. Slowly Molly raised her head, and the look that had come into her eyes at last was one that Bowyer had seen in the eyes of many men and women before. He knew that the time of his triumph had come.

'Unless I marry you, Tom Bowyer,' said Molly, 'you will betray my father, who trusted you?'

'I'll give him up to justice,' Bowyer shouted. 'I'll fight with what weapons I've got. My God, Molly, isn't it all part of the game? Wouldn't any man who was a man fight for what he wanted most of all in the world? If you don't give up, I swear he'll hang. You know what Canadian law is. I swear to you I'll have him hanged in Yorkton inside of six months if you don't agree to what I'm asking of you. It isn't as if you and Will Carruthers were engaged now,' he went on brutally.

'And if I do agree?' asked Molly, shuddering.

The sudden glance of hope in the factor's eyes went to her heart. But McDonald, crushed under his servitude, had a flicker of manhood after all.

'*Don't do it*, Molly, lass!' he shouted. 'I'll hang!' He turned upon Bowyer. 'I'll hang!' he shouted; and then his voice broke into a whimper.

'Shut up, you old fool!' said Bowyer contemptuously. 'If you agree, Molly,' he said, 'the past will all be forgotten. I swear it will. I love you, and I'll be true to you. I'll give you everything you want, and I'll make McDonald a home as long as he lives. Damn it! You look as if I was asking something awful of you! What's the matter with me? Ain't I good enough for you?'

Another silence followed. The factor's eyes were fixed on Molly's, and they seemed to contain all that there was of life in the white face, drawn like a death-mask, and set in innumerable, graven lines.

'Let me think!' cried the girl, pressing her hands to her eyes to shut that picture out.

And she thought with all the energy at her command, Will was gone out of her life. That left her nothing. She did not believe that the law would hang her father, but at least it would imprison him until he died. And she knew that his awful fear was hardly at all of death.

It was of the grave beneath the tamaracks, by which his own would never be dug; it was the impending fall of that blow which he had shrunk from all those years.

She looked up, to see Bowyer's red face peering into her own. She shivered, as if with mortal cold.

'I'll marry you,' she said.

The slow smile that spread over Bowyer's face was indescribable. He turned to McDonald. 'Well, that's settled at last,' he said, rubbing his hands together in gloating self-satisfaction. 'Get to bed, McDonald! Molly and I will sit up a while and talk over the details of our honeymoon trip. That ain't your business. Maybe we'll do a little love-making on the side, too, but not too rough. I guess I know how to handle a girl!'

He strode toward the door and opened it. The factor stood stock-still for a moment. Then, at Bowyer's call, he stumbled toward it, and Bowyer led him across the passage into another room.

'You'll be comfortable in here, McDonald!' Bowyer shouted, slapping the old man on the back. 'There's your bed, and I'll bring you your hot water in the morning.' He laughed boisterously. 'And don't you fear for Molly. I'll take mighty good care of her.'

There followed his returning footsteps, and the sharp, sudden click of a key. Then came a furious rattling from within. Bowyer turned angrily.

'Go to bed, you old fool!' he shouted. 'Didn't I tell you I'd take care of her?'

The rattling ceased, but Molly heard the factor's feet shuffling as he stood irresolutely behind his door, listening. Bowyer came back and slammed the door behind him. He put his hand on Molly's shoulder.

'Sit down, my dear,' he said, pointing toward the divan.

Molly obeyed. He took his seat beside her, and flung his arm over the back. She shrank from him with an instinct that she could not control, and she saw a spasm of anger cross Bowyer's face.

'I'm glad that's all settled at last,' he said. 'God, you've led me a chase, Molly! Hardest I've ever had; but I knew I'd get you in the end. I always do. Maybe I'd have got you, anyway, eh, my dear?' he continued, placing his red hand upon her white one.

'When do you wish me to marry you?' asked Molly in a whisper.

Bowyer threw back his head and laughed. 'Now you're talking,' he answered. 'That's the point I was coming to. I'm a business man, and I'm used to paying what I have to for what I want. Sometimes I have to pay more than I want. Sometimes prices go up — or down. Not that I'm meaning you, you understand. But I've been thinking that when two people are agreed on the same thing, and there's no way out of it, unless you want the old man to swing — why, it mightn't be necessary for you and me to get married at all.'

He slid his arm about her waist and bent his red face toward hers. For an instant the girl misunderstood. Then she leaped to her feet, her eyes blazing.

'Get out of my way, Tom Bowyer! If you try to stop me I'll murder you!' she screamed.

She ran round behind the divan,

snatched up the empty rifle, and, as Bowyer followed her, brought down the stock with all her strength.

Had it struck his skull it would have knocked him unconscious. But in the nick of time he leaped aside, and it fell across the muscles of his neck and shoulders. With a howl of pain he wrenched the weapon from her hands. He beat her across the face again and again with his fists. He seized her by the hair, twining it in his hand, and, forcing her head back, put his hands over her mouth.

She tried with all the strength she possessed to pry his hands away; the red and swollen face that leered into her own seemed to fill all space, like a huge, evil sun. Her cries were mingled with the shouts of the factor, who was rattling wildly at his door. With all the strength that remained in her she tore at the red hand over her mouth, and bit into it until her assailant yelled with pain. His grasp on her throat loosened for an instant. She drew in a deep gasp of air. Then she saw that the door was open.

Hackett was in the room. He was

shouting to Bowyer, who released the half-conscious girl, stood up, and yelled in answer. The outlaw was tugging frantically at his arm. There came the plunge of a heavy body against the door of the camp. Hackett sprang forward, and fell sprawling back under a terrific blow.

Wilton stood on the threshold.

25

Under Arrest

Molly saw it all as if in a dream. The hideous presence of her assailant was still with her. Then she saw Hackett and Bowyer pull pistols from their pockets. And each act was extended in her mind and vision through an eternity, as if it would never end.

She sprang to the table, seized the oil lamp, and hurled it at their backs.

It struck them fairly, sending them staggering before they had time to fire. Instantly the curtains before the window were ablaze. A stream of burning oil shot across the floor to the divan, which began burning furiously, filling the room with smoke. Wilton and the two men closed.

There followed a furious struggle. The combatants rolled over and over, stumbling against the burning divan, knocking over the chairs, crashing into the walls. All the while McDonald hammered at the door, and added his shouts to the uproar.

Molly darted across the passage and released him. 'They're murdering Will!' she cried. But the old man, staggering out, only shouted distractedly. Molly ran back. Hackett had Wilton by the throat, and, as she entered the room, Bowyer wrenched himself free, raised his pistol, and brought the butt crashing down on Wilton's head. Wilton toppled back into the blazing oil.

Bowyer aimed, but Molly knocked up his arm, and the shot went wild. Bowyer turned upon Molly with a ghastly grin.

'Damn you!' he shouted, raising his pistol to strike her down. McDonald sprang between them. Hackett pulled at Bowyer and dragged him to the door. He whispered in his ear, and Bowyer cursed him. They clinched in the passage.

Molly was unconscious of what was transpiring. She had rushed to Wilton, and, grasping him by the shoulders, pulled him out of the flames. Seizing him in her arms, she began madly beating out the fire that was licking his clothes and hair. She tore off his blazing coat and with it extinguished them. Then, holding his head against her breast, she staggered toward the door through the thick smoke, McDonald at her side.

As she neared it, Hackett leaped forward. He pushed the factor violently back and slammed it. An instant later there sounded the click of the key in the lock.

McDonald tugged at it desperately. They pulled together, but it held fast; and now the room behind them was a blazing furnace.

'The window! The window!' shouted the factor.

But that side of the room was a living wall of fire, and they seemed to be trapped hopelessly. The heat was becoming intolerable. McDonald's hair and beard were beginning to singe.

Molly ran behind the blazing divan, picked up the rifle, and drove a smashing blow against the back wall. It cracked; again and again she dashed the stock against it, until a section of the pine planks gave way under her assault.

Together they carried Wilton through

into a room behind. Outside it was quite light; a gust of wind came through an open window and fanned the flames to fury. With a roar the fire leaped up the outer walls, and the whole front of the camp was ablaze.

Molly scrambled to the sill, clung there, and dropped. The factor, leaning out, lowered Wilton's body. And he himself dropped to the ground beside the girl.

As he dropped she perceived, without realizing it, that he had used both arms and legs. The paralysis had left him.

They ran down toward the lake, carrying Wilton between them, and making instinctively for the shelter of the undergrowth.

As they passed the road, Bowyer came out of the stable, pulling fiercely at the horses, which were fastened to the rig. He had set his foot upon the step when Lee Chambers and Hackett broke upon him from among the trees.

They made a leap for the vehicle. 'Let us in, damn you!' Chambers yelled.

Bowyer dealt him a blow with the whipstock that sent him staggering. With a vile oath Hackett sprang for the step. Bowyer lashed him across the face, causing him to miss his footing, and cursing and shouting, the two men rushed after him and disappeared down the road. The sound of the galloping horses died away.

Molly kneeled at Wilton's side, bathing his face with water from the lake. The factor held his wrist.

'His pulse beats sound,' he said. 'He'll come back to himself soon. Let's awa', lass; let's awa'.'

The girl hardly heard him. Piteously she scanned Wilton's face for some signs of returning consciousness. But Wilton did not stir, though he was breathing easily.

Presently, with a hideous clamor, the two outlaws returned. Molly held her breath as they came back along the road, only a few yards above where she crouched with the factor. But they passed on, and turned up toward the camp, which blazed furiously, a flaming parallelogram against the glow of the eastern sky, into which the rim of the sun just projected from the horizon.

They had been drinking hard, for they

staggered and held each other, and shouted as they watched the sight. Presently, with one accord, they began to fire their pistols into the middle of the blaze. Molly heard Wilton's name and hers uttered. The ruffians had no idea that they had escaped, for there was no longer a broken wall between the rooms, nor any wall at all.

Even as she watched the girl saw the blazing walls tumble inward. The men leaped back, and then, shouting drunkenly, made their way toward the stables.

'Come awa', lass!' muttered McDonald, pulling at Molly's arm.

He took Wilton by the legs, and together they crept with him cautiously further into the bushes beside the lake. From here the uproar of the drunken ruffians in the stable could still be heard, but there was little likelihood of discovery.

Suddenly Wilton opened his eyes. And his first words fell like an icy chill on the girl's heart.

'Kitty, I tried to save your line!' he muttered.

He was thinking of the fire. He stared into Molly's eyes without recognition, and his own closed again. Once more the factor pulled at the girl's sleeve.

'Come awa', lass!' he whispered eagerly. 'He'll get well. Come! It's our chance — a grand chance for us!'

'What do you mean?' she whispered back.

'Dinna ye see? They think we're dead. Tom Bowyer'll think we're dead in the fire. He'll never trouble us again. Come, lass! He winna come to no harm!'

As he spoke, Molly perceived two horsemen riding along the road. They were policemen; they moved at a slow walking pace, and they carried their rifles on their arms. From where she crouched in the undergrowth she had a clear field of vision.

When they were within two hundred yards of the camp they dismounted, tied their horses to a tree, and began to run forward swiftly along the road. The uproar in the stable had not ceased. Hackett and Chambers, believing themselves secure, were making a day, as they had made a night of it.

Lee Chambers came staggering out, a bottle in his hand. And suddenly, a hundred yards away, he saw Quain and the constable.

He bolted back with a scream of terror. Then followed Hackett's bellowing roar, and the two men appeared at the door with rifles in their hands.

The policemen ran toward them. Quain led the way. 'Drop those! Hands up! We've got you!' he shouted.

They fired together in answer, with shaking hands that sent their bullets harmlessly overhead. Quain shouted again for their surrender. Molly saw Hackett drop to one knee and draw a careful bead upon the inspector.

At that moment the constable fired. The outlaw toppled head over heels like a shot rabbit, and never stirred again. The bullet had pierced his heart.

With a cry of despair, Chambers fired wildly and turned to run. Once more Quain shouted, and the constable fired again. Chambers dropped in his tracks and lay still.

Horror-stricken at the sight, Molly crouched by Wilton's side. His eyes were open again. He did not yet recognize her, but it was evident that consciousness was coming back to him.

As the policemen began to carry the bodies of the outlaws into the stable the factor plucked violently at Molly's arm.

'Lass, ye'll come with me now,' he pleaded. 'Dinna ye understand? We're dead — we're dead forever. It's our chance to begin our new life — the life we spoke about together.'

She saw that her father was verging upon a frenzy. And she understood the madness of his desire to shake off that past that had oppressed him so many years — the fear of Bowyer, always gnawing at his heart.

'What do you want to do, Father?' she whispered.

'I'll tell ye, lass. Ye ken the trail that strikes off from the road below the lake and runs nigh the portage? We'll tak' that. There'll be nobody about. And, ye see, lass, the police will stay here all day until they get a cart to carry the bodies back to Big Muskeg. Or maybe one of them will ride, but he winna go to the store. We'll go to the store and pack our few things and go. Aye, we'll go. We'll travel east through the bush twa hundred miles or maybe more, till we strike the line somewhere. And then we're free. I've five hundred dollars put awa' in the store for just such a circumstance. Dinna say no, lass!'

She was touched by the babbling, stammered words. They went straight to her heart.

'He's naething to ye, lass?' asked the factor, pointing at Wilton.

Molly looked at him. He had fallen into a deep sleep. She could do nothing for him by remaining.

'No, Father, he's nothing to me,' she answered.

'We'll put him a wee bit higher on the slope, where they'll see him,' the factor whispered.

They raised Wilton and laid him on the new fallen snow, not far from the road. Then, cautiously and secretively, they turned and plunged into the depths of the underbrush.

It was two hours later when Wilton opened his eyes, to find himself lying in the stable. The inspector was standing at the door; the constable paced at his side.

Wilton looked at Quain with astonishment. He could remember nothing since his plunge into the burning building.

'Jack!' he called feebly.

Quain turned back from the door and stood beside him.

'What's happened to me? How did you get here, old man?'

Quain, who appeared to be struggling with some deep emotion, did not answer him.

'You know how I got here?' continued Wilton. 'They trapped Miss McDonald and her father — where is she, Jack?'

'They're not here, Will.'

'They must be here. I tell you I saw her. That beast Bowyer had her by the throat. It made me see red! They got me down, and the place was afire, and — '

'Don't tell me that, Will,' said the inspector in a choked voice. 'Don't tell me anymore.'

'Why not, Jack? What's the matter with you?'

'Because you're under arrest for the willful murder of Joe Bostock. And I've — I've cautioned you!'

26

The Trap

Bob Payne, the lawyer, found himself in a quandary as he walked from his office toward the Clayton jail. He could not make up his mind whether his client, Will Carruthers, was innocent or guilty, and that was a position in which he did not often find himself.

Either Carruthers was one of the coolest and most deliberate murderers that had ever lived, or he was the victim of an extraordinarily well-woven conspiracy.

The former was the popular view. The groups that formed at the noon hour on Clayton's main street were unanimous in that belief, and, because Joe Bostock had been a universal favorite, the cry for a quick trial and speedy retribution was unanimous.

Only one man stood out against this expressed opinion. That was Jim Betts. But Jim was a cross-grained, queer character, and the very fact of his opposition only served to confirm the judgment of the few waverers.

Whether Wilton was innocent or guilty, Bob Payne meant to fight to the last. It was his first big case, and it had attracted attention throughout the Province. Besides, Payne had taken a liking to Carruthers, and he was resolved to free him. That, of course, presumed his own belief in his client's innocence. But Payne had set his mind that way in the face of the evidence, and his mind was the trained servant of his will.

The most damning thing in Payne's eyes was the fact that Wilton had once come to him with the purpose of weaving just such a web about Phayre.

He found his client seated in his cell, scribbling upon pieces of paper covered with diagrams, just as he had found him on the occasion of his previous visit. Wilton rose and they shook hands.

'That isn't connected with your case, Carruthers?' asked the lawyer, looking at the papers, his curiosity aroused.

'No,' answered Wilton. 'It's just some

plans of mine.' Then, seeing that Payne was evidently interested, 'I'm trying to work out a route for an extension of the Missatibi.'

Wilton's stock took a sudden tumble in Payne's estimation. Wilton was overdoing it. No man could feel as cool as that with a charge of murder hanging over his head.

Suddenly Wilton swept the papers to the floor. 'It's all I've got to do, Payne!' he cried. 'It's all that I can do to keep me from thinking! It's all that holds me back from going mad, with the memory of that night, and Molly — and Miss McDonald burned to death! You knew that we were once engaged to be married?'

Wilton's stock ran up again and reached a higher point than ever before. If Payne had graded his faith on a thermometer, it would have hovered above the line: 'Certainly innocent.'

He put his hand on Wilton's shoulder. 'I understand,' he said. 'But she may not be dead. Remember that nothing — no remains were found under the ruins.'

'She was there. I saw her, Payne. And now — she's gone. There isn't a chance she could have escaped. Where would she have gone if she had, except back to the store? That blaze would have destroyed all traces. The place was a furnace.'

'You escaped,' said the lawyer. 'How could you if she couldn't?'

Wilton clenched his fists. 'That's what's driving me mad,' he answered. 'How? I don't know, Payne. The only possible thing that I can think of is that, while half-conscious, I automatically fought my way out of the camp and left her and the old man to die in the fire.'

'I don't believe that, Carruthers. It isn't possible.'

'Why isn't it possible?'

'Because psychologists will tell you that when a man is half-conscious or delirious the real man comes uppermost. If you were that sort of man, and could control your cowardice by will-power — then, when the will had ceased to ride the body, yes, you might have done it. But there isn't a yellow streak in your nature.'

And this was a great deal for the lawyer to have vouched for. He was surprised afterward when he remembered that he had said that. Perhaps his real opinion had come uppermost in him.

He sat down. 'Let's go over the facts together,' he said. 'There's going to be a fight. You realize that? Not that you won't win out. Of course you will. But when popular passions are stirred — when a newspaper campaign has practically pre-judged the case, it's apt to be reflected in the minds of the jury. I've thought of asking for a change of venue. But — I'm frank, Carruthers — the feeling is widespread, and Clayton is the town where your enemies have the least influence. I think we'll fight them here.'

'I'll fight it out here,' answered Wilton.

'Well, now, we've got to meet the points they'll raise. First of all, it's no good laying emphasis on the fact that you were Joe Bostock's friend for years. That's what the prosecution is playing on.

'You want me to take the line that the whole conspiracy was trumped up by Bowyer and Phayre. Well, we've got to make sure of our ground before we can take it. We're on the defensive, Carruthers. And sometimes it's better to hold a strong position than to stake all upon a rash assault. There are just two things to consider: what can we prove against them, and what can they prove against us?

'There's no evidence whatever against Bowyer. I haven't the shadow of a doubt that he was at the back of the conspiracy to destroy your trestling and burn your camp, and play havoc with the Missatibi in general. And no doubt he wanted to find out what was in your safe. Those checks may have been forged by interested parties and put there. But it doesn't link up with Joe Bostock's death as the facts against you do link up with it. He had no motive. Do you see?'

Wilton listened and nodded. 'Go on,' he said.

'Your luck has been infernal. If it could be proved that Bowyer hired those men to kidnap Miss McDonald and her father — though it wouldn't help directly — it would create a prejudice in the minds of the jury. We could bring that in as evidence. It would discredit Bowyer. It would force him into the witness-box and give us an opportunity. If those men — if Miss McDonald could go into the witness-box — we could present something of a case. But they're dead — at least those outlaws are dead — and their secret died with them.'

'We can get Tonguay there.'

'I wouldn't hope for much.'

'He'll be scared to death. He can be made to speak.'

'You don't consider that he may be a star witness for the prosecution, Carruthers? He's got his neck to save. And, if your implication of Phayre is the correct one, you remember that Phayre is a director in the Clayton Hospital, and donated a large sum of money to it. Three weeks in a private room there offer opportunities.'

'You do believe that Phayre is implicated?' cried Wilton.

'I do, Carruthers. I'll be frank with you. I didn't at first. But I'm convinced that either Phayre or Bowyer was privy to Joe Bostock's murder. I believe it was an accident, and that they're playing on it to get you convicted.

'That's what we can prove against

them, and it amounts to nothing. Now what can they prove against us? You were Joe Bostock's friend. You knew all his affairs. You were his executor. For some reason or other Joe Bostock raised a loan of a large sum on five hundred Missatibi shares — probably to cover some other investment, and knowing that he could meet it when the time came. There's nothing abnormal or unusual about that.

'The money disappeared. No trace of it was to be found, and the presumption is that it went to certain Mexican centers that are now cut off from communication with the world owing to revolution. But — checks aggregating four hundred thousand dollars signed by Joe Bostock and made out in your favor are found in your safe. It is claimed that you presented them; that they passed through the bank in the normal way, and that they went back to you at the time you signed the monthly statement as his executor. The bank's books have been examined by order of court and found correct. As you frequently handled large sums of money for Mr. Bostock during his absence, this excited no suspicion at the time.

'You are presumed to have cashed those checks. Two days later you went into the bush with Mr. Bostock. He died at your side. Do you see the implication, as a juryman would see it?'

'And you believe I forged those checks?'

'I do not,' said Payne emphatically. 'But — I'll be frank — I couldn't see — '

'Then it was Phayre.'

'Phayre or Clark. The cashier, Bramwell, is only a boy. He's beyond suspicion. But Clark has a first-rate record. He was twelve years with the Regina branch of the Western National. We haven't been able to trace anything to his discredit. Still, there's not the least doubt Phayre and Bowyer fixed up this scheme to get control of the Missatibi and ruin you, at the best. Joe Bostock's death fitted in only too well with their purposes. But how those checks got into your safe, Carruthers — '

'Chambers placed them there, of course. I went over the papers immediately. I discovered that the safe was open, but the checks were the last thing I should have thought of looking at. I thought they were after the blueprints of the townships.'

'Then Chambers must also have abstracted the checks showing how Joe Bostock expended that five hundred thousand, and left those in their place. It's a diabolical contrivance, and I'm afraid we can't hope to make much impression with such a story on a jury, Carruthers. We'll have to approach the matter from an altogether different angle. Are you positive that you closed the safe?'

'I am absolutely sure, because I always tried it after closing, and made sure that the combination was not set.'

'It couldn't be opened without the combination?'

'Impossible. Of course, I'm not saying what mightn't be done by a master-craftsman — '

'But Chambers wasn't a burglar. He was an engineer, and always had been. He was a skilled one, too. He could do better by his profession than by burglary. That's the heaviest item in the prosecution's bill, Carruthers. It establishes a strong motive. That's what I mean when I say that we're on the defensive. It's no use ringing the changes on Bowyer's enmity or his desire to get the Missatibi. We can't prove anything on him, and he's in danger of proving much on you. The thing we have to do is to clear up this forgery situation.'

He hesitated. 'Carruthers, I'll be frank with you,' he said. 'There's another motive almost as strong. It's Mrs. Bostock.'

Wilton started; and then, realizing the infernal nature of the trap, he laughed grimly.

'She went to live at Big Muskeg — in an isolated cottage near your own — right after her husband's death. A damning thing in the eyes of men of the world, as all jurymen pride themselves on being. If we could show her interest was in the line, and not in you — that you weren't fond of each other before Joe Bostock died — '

'She was like a sister to me for Joe's sake,' said Wilton.

'Which is the last — *the very last suggestion* that I would put before a jury,' answered Payne.

Wilton had another visitor that day. It was Jim Betts, who had somehow obtained a permit to see him, and appeared outside the bars, accompanied by the warder.

'Will,' he said huskily, 'we're going to get you out of here. I told you them two snakes would be found at the bottom of the brushwood. I believe in ye, boy! That ain't much, maybe, but I want ye to know it.'

Wilton was deeply moved. 'Thank you, Jim,' he said warmly.

'And listen, boy! Ye remember how ye came to me about meeting that note when it falls due? I told ye I couldn't help ye. Well, boy, I was lying. I told ye ye'd best make terms with Phayre. If ye'd done that — well, I'd have kept my money. But ye didn't. Ye had the guts to go ahead and fight a battle that gave ye no more chance than a mouse in a cat's claws. And then I knew ye couldn't fail, and that my money'd be safer with you than in the best gilt-edged bonds that was ever put out.

'I was trying ye, Will, and ye've made good; and I want to say' — the old man's voice almost failed him — 'I want to say the money's yours to meet that note when it falls due, and I — I want ye to know this when ye're in trouble, and not when ye're out of it and all the world's slapping ye on the back and cheering ye, and — and — damn it, I'm going to get ye out of here a free man, or my name ain't Betts!'

27

Confession

When Wilton was arrested Kitty had been stunned by the news. She had made frantic attempts to see him, but without success. Then she had gone to Payne and begged him to take charge of the defense, offering to do all in her power, irrespective of expense, because of Wilton's friendship with Joe.

Payne, who, in common with everyone, had believed in Wilton's guilt when the facts were skillfully given out through Bowyer's agency, had been moved by her faith in the accused man. This had given him his first doubts. He had thought Kitty was actuated only by her own faith in Wilton; it was not until later that he began to suspect a warmer motive.

For days Kitty remained at home prostrated. She knew on what the charge was built, and the consciousness that

Wilton's freedom could only be purchased by her confession caused her an
agony of shame and fear. Yet she would
have purchased Wilton's freedom even at
the cost of that humiliation, had she not
known that she must inevitably lose him.
Instinctively she realized that treachery
was the one sin that he would never
condone.

And the news of the death of Molly
and her father was a further horror. What
might not have happened in the camp
during those hours before the fire?
Perhaps worse things than the awful
death that followed. For days she was ill
in bed, a prey to every torment of the
soul.

At last, when she could bear it no
longer, she resolved to go to see Bowyer.
Abhorrent though the journey was, it
seemed to her to offer the only possible
remedy. She left secretly, at an early hour
one morning, and reached Cold Junction
a little before noon.

At the same hour Bowyer was seated in
the office of his house there. Facing him
across the desk was Clark, the manager of

the bank of New North Manitoba at Clayton.

'Why d' you come to me?' jeered Bowyer, trying to fight down his burning rage. 'Why don't you go to Phayre?'

'I never go to the little men,' said Clark suavely. 'Not when there's bigger ones handy.'

'I'm not going to take you up on your preposterous story,' Bowyer stormed. 'I won't answer it. Nor will I deny it. You won't get 'yes' or 'no' out of me. Let's say you've rendered special and confidential services to the bank this past year and you want a bonus. How'll that do?'

'Call it what you like,' said Clark. 'But get me straight, Mr. Bowyer. I didn't tackle that job to be fobbed off with a paltry two hundred dollars. I know what it was worth to you and I want a proper price for it.'

Bowyer, who knew how to handle men, made him no offer, but, picking up his checkbook, wrote out a check for a thousand dollars. He blotted it and handed it to Clark, who looked at it and smiled. Bowyer had not gaged Clark.

'I may as well tell you,' said Clark. 'I'm not bargaining. I'm going to bleed you just what you're willing to stand. One hundred and fifty thousand dollars in bonds, which I'll specify, and fifty thousand in cash.'

Bowyer went white. Clark had gaged his limit exactly. The two men eyed each other in silence for a few seconds. Then Bowyer capitulated.

'Your talents are wasted here,' he said. 'I'll take you up on that, and I'll be able to employ you to better advantage after the first of the year. You're not afraid of a check?'

'Not in the least,' said Clark. 'I'll have that list of bonds for you a little later. I'm waiting to see how Pequonsets Consolidated move. Thank you!'

He took the check and sauntered out of the house. When he was gone Bowyer gave way to one of his mad rages. He called up Phayre and damned him. He stamped up and down the office; and in the middle of it his man announced Kitty.

When she came in he was smiling and admirably under control. He offered her a chair and looked in admiration at her blue eyes and clear skin. In the past Bowyer had been afraid of Kitty; now that he had her in his power he scented a new pursuit.

'Well, Mrs. Bostock, I guess this isn't social,' he said. 'Last time we parted you were quite vexed with me.'

Kitty put her hands to her eyes and broke down. 'I can't bear it,' she sobbed. 'It's too awful! I've been ill for days, and — I had to come to you. It's Wilton and Molly. If you had any hand in that poor child's death, may God forgive you, Tom Bowyer!'

Bowyer winced. In his joy at having escaped before the police arrived upon the scene, he had managed to smother his conscience tolerably well, especially when he reflected that Molly had herself started the fire. Besides, it was Hackett who had taken alarm and pulled him from the room when he might have saved her.

'Make yourself easy,' he said sullenly. 'I hadn't any hand in it. I don't know what happened, but I guess she didn't go to the camp against her will, Mrs. Bostock,' he leered. 'Maybe she'd taken a fancy to Lee Chambers. I saw something of that sort in the wind, and so I hadn't started to carry out our plan.'

'Our plan!' gasped Kitty.

'The one that we agreed on, to keep her away from Will Carruthers,' said Bowyer venomously.

He expected an outburst, but Kitty was beyond that now. 'You know that I've come about Will,' she said in a choking voice. 'I don't know what to do. Nobody but you can help me. What shall I do?'

Bowyer pretended to reflect. 'I don't quite see what you can do, Mrs. Bostock,' he answered. 'I don't believe he's guilty — '

'Of course he isn't guilty!'

'I've always said he isn't. But he'll have to take his verdict from the jury. They won't convict unless they're pretty dead sure. If they do, it'll be on good evidence. What is there we can do?'

Kitty looked at him in consternation. 'The safe!' she gasped. 'That's what — '

'But that has nothing to do with Joe's death, Mrs. Bostock.'

She sprang to her feet, confronting him with dramatic indignation. 'You know that it has everything!' she cried. 'You're playing with me and torturing me. Do you suppose I don't know what they're saying about him — that he forged Joe's name to those checks and murdered him to prevent discovery? Do you suppose I don't know that, when I gave you the combination, just to help Will, that you put those checks there? Let me tell the truth on the witness stand!' she pleaded, standing before him with clasped hands, and the tears raining down her cheeks.

'Tell the truth? You must be mad!' he shouted.

'If the jury knew that, they'd acquit him. It could be arranged. I'd say I gave the combination to Lee Chambers — '

Again Bowyer began to be afraid of Kitty; but this time it was her stupidity he feared. For he understood her at last: a woman's heart, a schemer's brain, and a child's mind and experience — that was Kitty Bostock.

And he saw that this was the occasion to let loose one of his habituated rages.

He seized her hands in his, one in each, and twisted them until she screamed with the pain.

'Let's understand each other, Kitty Bostock!' he hissed in a furious voice. 'I'll take up your proposition and show you what it means. Listen! First, you'll break your solemn covenant with me. Dishonest, you think? The sort that's made between people every day. I've played fair with you. And you'll play fair with me, or you'll lose your fortune — every penny of it. That's first.

'Second, so surely as you go into the witness-box with such a story I'll say you lie. I'll say he was your lover. I'll say that he killed Joe at your instigation because you wanted to be rid of him. I'll say that you went to Big Muskeg and lived there, almost next door to him. I'll bring forward a workman who saw you two together, kissing on the swamp one evening. You thought that little scene wasn't overheard and noticed, did you? I'll swear it's a concocted story made up by you to free your paramour. What sort of figure do you think you'll cut in the witness-box then, Kitty Bostock?'

Bowyer had calculated rightly. Upon a woman like Kitty, petted and spoiled from birth, the astounding fact of physical violence comes as a stunning shock that breaks down the soul's resistance. It is only on repetition that the reaction comes.

And Bowyer calculated rightly again. He dropped her hands and stood looking at her as one who has suffered wounding in the house of a friend.

'Kitty Bostock,' he said gently, 'I promise you that he shall be freed. I have the means, the influence, the power. I didn't guess that suspicion of Joe's death would fall on him. I know he didn't murder Joe. Keep your head, and all shall be well. I swear it. Do you believe me?'

She looked at him as if he had hypnotized her. 'Yes, I believe you,' she answered.

'So surely as you speak one word, he'll hang. Keep quiet, and he shall be saved. Promise me you'll say nothing!'

'Oh, I'll say nothing,' wailed Kitty, wringing her hands. 'I promise you. I see.

Yes, I understand now.'

And she went out of the house with her head low, dubious, and yet with the sure conviction that Bowyer could save Wilton. Bowyer could save him, but nobody else could do so. She would trust him, because there was nobody else to trust.

When she had gone, Bowyer sank back in a chair and wiped his forehead. He had had two blows that day, and, notwithstanding his habitual poise, he felt the solid ground trembling beneath him.

He had been sure Kitty would come to him, and he had been sure he could make her see what he had made her see. But he had never guessed Kitty was such a fool — or had so much heart and conscience, which, in his opinion, came to about the same thing.

Between the house and the station Kitty grew conscious of an old man walking beside her, trying to speak to her. Absorbed in her thoughts, she did not know how long he had been there. Suddenly she realized that this was Jim Betts.

She shrank back aghast, looking at him

with eyes wide with fear. Jim nodded and smiled.

'It's all right; don't be afeared of me, Mrs. Bostock,' he said. 'You're mighty worried about Will, ain't you now? I guess we all are.

'And you've been to see Tom Bowyer, to ask him to help you and Will? That snake won't help you, child. It ain't his nature. Will didn't murder Joe, nor steal his money, neither; but things look mighty black for him, and he's in a bad way. Won't you go to Mr. Payne and tell him what you know?'

'What do you mean?' cried Kitty shrilly. 'I don't know anything, except that Will's innocent.'

'Tell Mr. Payne that, Mrs. Bostock,' persisted Jim.

'He knows it. What is there for me to tell? You're trying to trap me — all of you.'

'No, Mrs. Bostock, we ain't trying to trap you,' said Jim doggedly. 'We're trying to save Will. Don't you suppose we're better friends to Will than Tom Bowyer is?'

They had reached the station. The train for Clayton was waiting. Jim followed Kitty into the compartment and took his seat beside her. Presently they were off, grinding out the miles across the dreary snowbound waste. Kitty sat silent beside Jim, who watched her face in quiet eagerness.

She was trying to find some guidance, and her mind was all awhirl. Could she trust Bowyer? Could anyone help her? Why had Jim Betts found her in Cold Junction and followed her? Why was he persecuting her?

'Jest think, Mrs. Bostock, what would Joe have done if he'd known Will was in trouble?' pleaded Betts. 'Would he have gone to Tom Bowyer to ask him to save him?'

Suddenly Kitty broke down in tears. 'I don't know what to do,' she sobbed. 'I'll do anything — anything for Wilton. But I don't know how to do it.'

'You said I was trying to trap you, Mrs. Bostock. Then there must be something to trap. You'd know something about all this if anybody did. Tell me. I won't tell nobody. I'll let Will go to the gallows rather than tell, unless you let me.'

She blanched and turned a glance of terror upon him. 'He'll be acquitted!' she cried. 'It's absurd! Nobody'll believe such an accusation.'

'No, Mrs. Bostock, he'll be convicted sure, unless we can get to the bottom of it all,' said Jim.

'Tom Bowyer swore he'd save him if — if — '

'If — ' questioned Jim.

'If I keep silent. But I'll speak. I will. I never trusted him. Mr. Bowyer told me I couldn't hold the line, and I wanted to save the money to help Will. He promised that when the smash came he'd take the shares off my hands at par if I'd give him the combination of the safe, so that he could find out about the plans. I gave it to him. The safe was mine — and I was trying to help Will. And I told Tom Bowyer the secret of the wheat lands, so that he'd know he wasn't losing anything by buying my shares.'

She let her head fall, against Jim's shoulder, sobbing uncontrollably. Jim laid his rough hand on her hair.

'There, child, I guess you feel better now, don't you!' he said. 'You didn't understand the wrong that you were doing. That's the way wrong's generally done. And now we'll go to Mr. Payne and fix things up for Will.'

28

The Closing of the Trap

Payne had not admitted to Wilton how serious the situation was. If it could be shown that the bank had forged Joe's transfer of the shares; if it could be proved that the checks were forgeries, and had been deposited in the safe in Wilton's absence, the tables would be turned, and one of the two props of the prosecution knocked from under it. Otherwise —

Sometimes again Payne found himself wondering whether his client was really innocent, after all.

Then he beat down his doubts and set his mind to work. He had suspected that Kitty could furnish him with a clue, but he had been able to elicit nothing from her.

He was struggling with his perplexities about a month before the date set for the trial when Jim Betts and Kitty came to his office. They had gone there from the station, and, with quivering lips and in trembling voice, Kitty sobbed out her story, while Payne listened in utter amazement.

'Why did you do this, Mrs. Bostock?' he asked, when he had heard her to the end.

'Because I love Will and wanted to help him,' she answered.

'You are willing to tell that story in the witness-box just as you've told it to me?'

'I will!' cried Kitty. 'If it will save Will — if it's needed to save him.'

Jim Betts looked at Payne. 'I guess that clears him,' he said hopefully.

The lawyer shook his head. 'I'll put her in the box as a last resource, if I must,' he answered. 'But not unless I must.'

'Why, ding it, won't that clear him?' shouted Betts.

'I'm afraid, Mr. Betts, that it will not,' said Payne. 'Tom Bowyer's clinched his case; and of all his damnable rascalities the way he's got Mrs. Bostock into his power's the worst. Would you believe that story if you were a juryman? However, I'll try it if I must. Meanwhile, we mustn't stop looking round for another point of attack.'

★   ★   ★

He did not find one. As the day of the trial drew nearer he knew Will's case was desperate. Public opinion was inflamed against him, and Bowyer's skillful campaign had borne rich fruits. The courtroom was packed to suffocation. Only one juror was challenged; he had been an employee of Bowyer's once, and, as it was learned, he was the one man, apart from Betts, who had proclaimed his belief in Wilton's innocence.

This was a bad omen, but the outlook became more ominous as the trial progressed. The prosecution established the fact that Joe and Wilton had been absolutely alone at the time of the murder. Indian witnesses deposed that the dead outlaws had been peddling liquor in their camp, miles from the scene, at the same hour. Papillon and Passepartout, placed in the box, swore that they had not left

328

their encampment until the afternoon, expecting Joe and Wilton to return.

Without animus, but in the resolve to clear his own reputation for laxity, Quain had worked up the case until each link appeared complete. Andersen, who followed the Indian witnesses, testified reluctantly that he had overheard Wilton request the pseudo policemen to delay their journey to Clayton, as he did not wish Joe Bostock's death to be known, for business reasons, until sometime later. There followed an expert in medical jurisprudence.

'Would it be possible for one man to shoot another through the heart from behind, and at the same time to have his left arm shattered by the bullet?' asked Payne.

'If they were standing face to face, and he put his right arm round the other and fired obliquely, that would be a quite likely result,' answered the expert.

'Could it be done with a rifle?'

'No. It could be done with an automatic pistol.'

'From your examination of the remains, would you say that the wound was inflicted by a pistol or a rifle bullet?'

'It is quite impossible to say.'

'What caliber bullet would pierce a man's body and still have force enough to break another man's arm?'

'A .450, fired at close range, provided it passed clean through the heart between the ribs.'

Payne cross-examined other witnesses to elicit the fact that Wilton had possessed no automatic, but he produced no impression by it.

There followed Papillon and Jean Passepartout, who stated that they had been told by the outlaw Hackett, that Wilton had murdered Joe Bostock. Having already come to the same opinion, and being afraid of having the guilt laid to them, they had decided to run away.

The next witness was Tonguay, who deposed that he had been peddling liquor at the Indian camp at the time of the tragedy. Having learned of it from the Indians, who had got the news from Papillon and Passepartout, the two men had formed the plan of impersonating policemen and arresting Wilton, in order to blackmail him. It was their intention to hold him to ransom in a hiding-place nearby, where they kept their stolen uniforms, until the money arrived.

'Subsequently you and Hackett went to the camp again to peddle liquor?' asked the crown attorney.

'Hackett told me there was a good chance to make money there, and I went wit' heem.'

'Did you ever make the acquaintance of an engineer named Chambers?'

'Sure!' grinned Tonguay.

'What was Chambers doing there?'

'Oh, I guess he got a job.'

'Was that why he went there?'

'I guess he had somet'ing better than that,' said Tonguay.

'Did he tell you what it was?'

'He tole me he knew somet'ing about Mr. Carruthers what give him a pain in de neck to t'ink about, an' he got a job out of him, an' meant to get somet'ing more.'

To Payne's trained brain the man was speaking as if he had been coached, but the sensation caused by his words was indescribable. There was not the faintest stir in the courtroom as the crown attorney proceeded.

'Did he tell you what the nature of his hold was over the defendant?'

'How's dat?' stammered Tonguay.

'Did he say what Mr. Carruthers had done?'

'He didn't say dat. He said he done somet'ing what give him a pain in the neck,' repeated Tonguay artlessly. 'And he say we stan' in together an' get somet'ing more out of him.'

Payne leaped to his feet as Tonguay ended his evidence.

'Who told you to tell that story?' he shouted. 'Did you learn that while you were in the hospital?'

Tonguay rolled his eyes, gulped, and blinked. Taken aback, he did not know what to say.

'I object to the insinuation!' shouted the crown attorney.

Suddenly the courtroom broke into a cheer. The suppressed excitement rippled from bench to bench, and was caught up by the crowds outside, ignorant though they were of its meaning. The sounds fell like lead on Payne's ears. Taken aback, he found the judge upholding the crown attorney's objection before he could regain his self-control.

'Do you know Mr. Bowyer?' he demanded, when the noise had subsided.

'I object again!' protested the crown lawyer.

'The witness may answer the question,' said the judge.

'What's dat you ask me? Sure I know Tom Bowyer. Everybody know him. He give me a job once, five, six year ago. I ain't seen him since den.'

As Payne nodded to him to go he heard a buzz of excitement in the courtroom. All eyes were turned toward the crown attorney, at whose side stood Bowyer himself; and it was evidently the intention of the prosecution to call him to the stand.

His eyes attracted upward suddenly, he saw Kitty, in her widow's black, seated in the front row of the gallery, her eyes fixed in terror upon the newcomer. And, as if drawn by the force of her will, Bowyer looked up, and Payne saw the flicker of a smile cross his red, vulpine countenance.

Payne's discouragement yielded to red-hot anger. He would show this fox no mercy. But before Bowyer's name had been called, a note, hastily scribbled by Wilton, was put into his hand. He opened it and read:

Remember, nothing about Miss McDonald.

He had been forced to promise that; and with that the nervous energy created by his anger went out of him, leaving him with a sense of hopelessness.

Bowyer, called, deposed that he had known Joe Bostock intimately for several years. They had always been friendly, though often business rivals.

'When did you first learn of his death?' asked the crown attorney.

'Not for several days after.'

'But you met the accused at the Hudson's Bay Company's store at Big Muskeg a few days after the event?'

334

'Two days after.'

'What were you doing there?'

'I was passing in a sleigh to look over some timber rights in the district.'

'What did he say to you about the tragedy?'

'He told me Joe Bostock was not with him.'

'And he said nothing about his death?'

'No. I knew nothing about it for two or three days after that.'

'What was the defendant's demeanor at the store?'

'Strange,' answered Bowyer. 'He appeared to be laboring under intense excitement. I spoke to him about the possibility of acquiring an interest in the Missatibi, and he assaulted me. He had a broken arm, and so I went away quickly without returning the blow.'

'Was his demeanor that of a guilty man?'

Payne leaped to his feet. 'I object to that question!' he shouted. But Bowyer was already answering:

'He looked like a man mad with fear.'

As he spoke he glanced upward. There came a scream from the gallery, and Kitty

335

fell back fainting, in her chair.

The court adjourned until the morrow. The mob that packed the streets was for the most part silent as Wilton was conveyed back to the jail, but hisses and hoots were heard. Payne went to his client almost immediately.

'What do you make of it all?' asked Wilton gravely.

Payne was silent awhile. It had gone worse than he had considered possible. Tonguay's perjured statement had made an intense impression upon all in the courtroom. Wilton's guilt seemed now to have been established by the strongest circumstantial evidence, as well as by the elimination of all others. That Chambers had guessed at it, had tried to blackmail Wilton, then to steal, and had killed Jules in the attempt, had been brought out severally by independent witnesses.

When Bowyer's evidence was done the third leg of the tripod would be set up — the motive for the crime. An array of handwriting experts was in waiting to prove the signature of the transfer genuine, and that of the checks a forgery.

But, apart from all this, Payne had the sense that every lawyer knows — the sense in anticipation of the jury's verdict. There was hardly a shadow of doubt.

'It looks bad,' answered Payne.

'They must have bought up Tonguay. I was a fool to hide Joe's death. Inquire for Kitty when you go back and try to let me know how she is, won't you? And tell her not to worry. Tell her I'm going to pull out triumphantly, for the sake of the line,' said Wilton.

Payne left him with the resolve to put Kitty upon the stand. He did not tell Wilton this. He would have avoided this had it been possible. But it was the only chance remaining. The jury might believe her. There was the bare possibility that they would. It would, of course, supply the prosecution with a second, and even stronger motive for the murder. But the prosecution might mean to call Kitty, anyway.

Suddenly there leaped into Payne's mind the overwhelming conviction that Bowyer was at the back of the murder. Nothing else could explain his vindictiveness. He had believed that Bowyer and

Phayre had utilized the death of Joe Bostock to perpetrate their fraud. Now he knew that Bowyer, at any rate, was guilty of being accessory to the greater crime. And that knowledge was the lawyer's sense, too.

He learned that Kitty was recovering, and, before returning to inform Wilton, he had the impulse to go to Jim Betts' quarters. He wanted to see the only man who still believed in Wilton's innocence, apart from the erratic juryman whom he had unfortunately challenged. He wanted to strengthen his own faith with Betts.

Jim Betts occupied a suite of rooms at the 'Clayton,' the one ornate hotel that the little town possessed. Payne thought it strange that he had not seen Betts for a long time, though he had been too busy to wonder before.

At the hotel he was told that the old man had left Clayton two weeks before and had not yet returned.

Payne made his way slowly back to the jail. He had to uphold his faith alone — his faith in an acquittal. It was the hardest job he had ever had in his life.

29

The Guilty Man!

The inquest on the bodies of Hackett and Lee Chambers had established the fact, ascertained by a search-party on the day after the fire, that there were no human remains under the charred timbers of the camp. Notwithstanding this, when the attempts made to trace McDonald and his daughter failed, it was generally believed that they had been lured there by the outlaws, and had either died in the flames or had been murdered and their bodies disposed of.

A party of the police had searched the neighborhood for days in this belief; and, under this belief, no systematic search had been made of the surrounding country, beyond the dispatching of wires to the towns along the roads and railroads.

Jim Betts had nothing more substantial

than anyone else on which to base his search. He was resolved to free Wilton; he realized the strength of the case against him, and, acting on his proverb that women did not mix with business, having failed with Kitty, he determined to discover the other woman who, he felt sure, had been mixed up in Wilton's life — if she still lived.

Jim Betts was the only man besides Payne who knew that Bowyer had actually been at the camp. Wilton had insisted that no mention should be made of this, for the sake of Molly. Payne had acquiesced on different grounds; he knew that no one would believe Wilton's statement, and that it would have a prejudicial effect on him as an attempt to incriminate a business rival.

Betts built up the theory that Wilton had arrived at the camp too late to save the girl from Bowyer, and that, half-crazed, she had fled with her father into the wilderness. He knew McDonald slightly, and the bent of his mind. McDonald would readily fall in with his daughter's aim. It was the most likely thing in the world that they had sought some of the isolated posts or missions in the great wilderness northward or eastward — if they were alive.

Betts had not struck silver by recognizing doubts. Once he had elaborated his theory, he acted as if it were true. He put off his town habit and became the prospector once more — rough, surly, trudging along the roads with his kit on his back, keen-eyed as a hawk and tireless and indefatigable as an Indian.

He went to the fishing camp and spent a day prowling among the ruins, but he learned nothing there. Then he went to the store. It was still empty, for a new trading post was being established northward, and the company had not replaced the factor, perhaps would not do so. Betts broke in.

Everything was as it had been on the night of the fire. But Betts quickly discovered that someone had been there since. For in the dust that covered the floor of Molly's bedroom were the faint imprints of feet. A woman's foot!

That was all the clue Betts got, but it

satisfied him. He cast about him, northward and eastward, going into every Indian encampment and talking with the inhabitants. But it was a week before he got his second clue.

* * *

Molly and her father left Wilton beside the road and crept stealthily into the undergrowth. When they were a sufficient distance from the camp they made a wide detour, crossed the road, and took the trail back toward the portage, encountering nobody on the way.

There the factor got his five hundred dollars, and made up a pack of food sufficient for a two weeks' journey. He took his rifle and ammunition, and a small canvas tent; they put on their snowshoes and started eastward.

It was their plan to travel two hundred miles to the Ontario border, then turn southward and strike the transcontinental line.

The snow fell heavily, but it was still late autumn, and they suffered little from the cold. At the end of the first day they had covered more than twenty miles. They felt safe from pursuit. They put up the tent, cooked their meal, and slept.

Molly had noticed that the factor's paralysis had completely left him. She said nothing to him about it, however, fearing to bring it to his attention. McDonald discussed their future ceaselessly. They would reach some town and rest; he would get a new job and, in the wilds, they would begin their life anew. Molly listened quietly. A new life for her — perhaps, after she had shaken off all the memories of the old. They traveled for eight days. On the eighth McDonald showed signs of weakness; he had overtaxed his strength, and he could hardly shoulder his pack when they went on the next morning.

They were following an Indian track that led to a little Moravian mission, twelve miles further on. They decided to push forward to it and rest there. When they reached it at nightfall, McDonald was in a raging fever and half-delirious.

The brother in charge welcomed them; he put the factor to bed and nursed him assiduously through a sharp attack of pleurisy. McDonald, in his delirium, raved incessantly. All the ghosts of the past tortured him. Out of his disconnected mutterings the girl at first could make little. Her mother, Joe Bostock, Bowyer, Wilton, made their exits and their entrances upon that phantom stage of his mind; but Molly could see that some central episode held that stage, and that they clustered round it.

Night after night he raved, while Molly tended him in his anguish. But at last the delirium left him, and conscience, screaming into the sick man's soul, could no more pass the seal upon his lips.

He lay silent now, and as sullen as before. At last the day came when he could leave his bed; and he would sit for hours in his chair before the stove, gazing out through the window. He was in a fever to be gone.

'Tomorrow,' was the constant burden of his plaint.

Molly began to fear that he would never get well unless his longing could be gratified. And yet his recovery was so slow; it was December now, and bitter cold. She spoke to the brother one day about a sleigh. When she told McDonald he burst into one of his frenzies. They would be caught in a sleigh; they must travel afoot along the trails.

'But we are not flying from anyone,' said Molly, wondering what it was that hounded him.

He wanted his rifle; he cleaned and oiled it. He asked for his snowshoes, and began examining the strings. As Molly gave them to him she suddenly perceived that one of the strings was broken. And there flashed into her mind the memory of her discovery beside the portage on that day when she saved Wilton.

She would not let the dark thought in her heart come into her consciousness. But she kneeled at the factor's side, her arms around him. 'What is troubling you?' she pleaded. 'Tell me! There's nothing you fear, is there? You are not troubling still about that man you killed so long ago? You've suffered enough for that. You've paid the penalty in full for that!'

345

He glowered at her, but she pressed him in her arms more closely.

'You must tell me, Father. We can't go on like this if we are to start our new life together. Tell me what's on your mind. We must have it out now, if we are to go on.'

McDonald was shaking like an aspen. 'It's naething, lass!' he babbled. 'If I've repaid, it's for wrong that was done me and mine.'

'What have you done? Whom have you repaid? You must tell me!'

He groaned. He clutched at her. 'I warned him what would be if ever he came between me and mine. And when he sent Will Carruthers to steal you from me — for he was at the back of that — I shot him.'

'Whom?'

Molly's gray eyes searched into his soul.

'Joe Bostock!'

After a long time Molly took the factor's hands in hers. 'We'll go on,' she said in a hard voice. 'Thank God, no innocent man has been suspected. I'll stay with you. I'll never speak of this again.

But if ever the guilt is unjustly placed on anyone, you will go back to Clayton and confess the truth, or I'll denounce you.'

'Aye, I'll go back, Molly!' he cried. 'No man shall hang for me. I swear it — if ye'll stay by me till then, Molly.'

She left him, and, with a singular clarity of mind, as if there were nothing more to fear or hope, and no room for further feeling, she went to the door and looked out across the snow-bound wilderness.

She saw a figure tramping through the falling snow toward the mission. And thus Jim Betts found her.

30

A Dramatic Moment

Contrary to public expectation, Bowyer's remaining evidence was not sensational, and Payne asked him only a few questions.

The rest of the second day was occupied by the handwriting experts — gentlemen brought to Clayton at fat fees, who unanimously testified that the signature on the transfer was genuine, and those on the checks forgeries. On the third day the defense opened, and Payne called Kitty, resolutely ignoring alike Wilton's signals, and the crown lawyer's satisfaction, and Bowyer's vulpine smile.

'The defendant was a friend of your husband?' he asked.

'My husband's greatest friend,' she answered.

'He brought his body back to Clayton under great difficulties, although his arm was broken?'

'Yes.'

'Who accompanied him on the journey?'

'Miss McDonald, of Big Muskeg portage.'

'You have reason to believe that they were engaged to be married at the time?'

'I had it from his own lips.'

'You nursed him during his following illness?'

'I did.'

'What was his attitude toward you and the Missatibi Company?'

'He wanted me to help him fight to hold it for me, on Joe's account.'

'And he asked you to come to Big Muskeg to live?'

'He tried to stop me. It was my suggestion, because I wanted to follow the work.'

Payne shot a fleeting glance at the jury. They were watching Kitty with unchanged faces; but there was no disbelief on them.

'At the portage you met Mr. Bowyer one evening, I believe?'

'Yes.'

'Tell us the conversation that ensued.'

'I caught him trying to embrace Miss McDonald. He told me that he loved her, and would win her from Will Carruthers.

349

He taunted me with being in love with Will. I was. *I am!'*

She drew herself up proudly and flung out the words with indescribable energy. The whole court was electrified by her words and manner. It staggered Payne. It was one of the worst things she could have said. He did not dare glance at the jury.

'What was the nature of the bargain that Mr. Bowyer offered?' continued the lawyer.

'He said he would win Miss McDonald and get her out of my way if I would help him gain control of the Missatibi. He told me that he would take my shares at their par value when the crash came, so that I could use the money to help Will Carruthers. And he asked me to give him the combination of the safe, so that he could examine some papers there. He said it was my safe, and I controlled the line, so that I would be doing no wrong.'

'What answer did you make?'

'I gave him the combination,' answered Kitty in a low voice.

A cry broke from Wilton's lips; he raised his arms and let them fall again.

There was an intense hush in the court, and then an excited murmur. Payne glanced at the jury. Their eyes were riveted on Kitty's face. He knew that he had scored. A disagreement — even an acquittal — if all went well.

'Thank you,' he said quietly.

The crown attorney, who had been whispering with Bowyer, came forward to cross-examine.

'You told us, Mrs. Bostock,' he said in his suavest tones, 'that you loved, and still love, the defendant. How long have you loved him?'

'Ever since I first saw him,' whispered Kitty.

'How soon after your marriage did you make his acquaintance?'

'I saw him first on my marriage day, at the church. He was my husband's best man. He traveled a hundred miles to act for him.'

Another stir among the spectators. Payne clenched his firsts and groaned. Everyone saw what was coming — everyone but Kitty.

'Then you were in love with him before

you married Mr. Bostock? Not long before — let us say half an hour? You married a man whom you had ceased to love for half an hour?'

'I didn't realize it then.'

'But you realized it soon after? You were not heartbroken when Mr. Bostock died? You did not feel your life was crushed and blighted?'

'I cared for Joe. I admired and respected him.'

'But not in the same way? You couldn't love two men in that way at the same time?'

'No,' said Kitty tremulously.

'In fact, after the first shock was over, you felt that life might become worth living again? You might even have welcomed your husband's death as offering you a deeper love?'

'I don't know what you mean!' cried Kitty desperately.

'The court will,' said the attorney with a meaning glance toward the jury. 'Don't let me perplex you. Now please answer me carefully. You persuaded the defendant to let you build and occupy a cottage at Big Muskeg, close to his own, and hidden from the sight of the camp?'

'He tried to stop me. I've said that already.'

'It has duly impressed us, Mrs. Bostock. However, in the end he yielded?'

'He yielded because he thought that I was only interested in the work. He cared for Miss McDonald. He never dreamed I cared, until I told him.'

'So you told him! What did he say?'

'It cut him to the heart.'

Only a thread divided the tense drama of the colloquy from inextinguishable bathos. The attorney snapped it.

'In short, you found him a regular Joseph in his relations with you?'

And the whole court was dissolved in laughter. The spectators roared; the jurors, at the sudden reversal, leaned back in their places, their faces convulsed. Even the judge placed his hand across his mouth.

'Then will you tell me how you two came to be seen kissing and embracing one evening on the shores of Big Muskeg? But I won't press that question. We shall have further evidence to offer.'

'Erase that question from the record!' ordered the judge.

But the mischief was done. The net that had been woven about Wilton could not be broken by the hypothesis of conspiracy. Kitty's confession of her love supplied a stronger argument against him, and threw the dark shadow of collusion about her, too. Mechanically Payne called his next witness.

But before he could take the stand there came sounds of an uproar in the street. There was a struggle at the entrance. Then, to the amazement of all, Molly stood in the doorway.

Jim Betts was with her, and together they supported the frail form of McDonald.

Unhindered, they went down the court-room, while the spectators gaped, and suddenly, standing up in their places, gave rousing, riotous cheers, unhindered and unrebuked.

Despite the general belief in Wilton's guilt, stories concerning Bowyer's presence at the camp on the night of the fire had been widely bruited. In their amazement at this resurgence from the dead the audience knew instinctively that events even more sensational were to follow.

The party were still advancing when Bowyer loosed himself in one of his paroxysmal rages.

'Put them out of here!' he bawled. 'It's a trick — a staged trick to win sympathy for that man!'

'Be silent!' thundered the judge; and then he turned to Payne, who was at his side, speaking in a low voice.

'The court will adjourn for half an hour,' he ordered. 'And no person will leave this courtroom in that interval.'

Instantly the eyes of all were riveted upon Bowyer, who, with Phayre and Clark, was making his way toward the nearest exit. They stopped and looked about them in confusion.

A thousand hands went out toward them. Yet no word came from the spectators. Those outstretched arms were like the mute judgment at the gladiatorial games, pronouncing sentence.

Bowyer snarled like a trapped fox, and sank into a seat. The crown attorney went to him hastily and sat down beside him. The two whispered together. It struck Payne as curious afterward that, in this sudden reversal of sympathy and opinion, no word had been uttered.

But Molly, with a little cry, ran to the dock and flung herself into Wilton's arms. And at this the building rang again and again with the spectators' cheers. It was not for a full minute that the guard drew her away.

31

The Amazing Truth

'Donald McDonald to the witness-box!' said the court clerk.

A chair had been placed there. Helped by Payne and the policeman, the old factor made his way painfully toward it and sat down.

Death was upon him; so meager and weak he looked that it seemed as if the man lived only in the impassioned fire of his eyes and the purpose that knit together his trembling body.

'You are acquainted with the circumstances of Joe Bostock's death?' asked Payne. 'Tell us what you know about it.'

'I killed him,' said McDonald simply.

Bowyer leaped to his feet; the crown attorney, turning, as if he had been prepared for the movement, pushed him down sharply into his chair. There was a moment's struggle, during which no word was spoken anywhere.

Then the story, at last unsealed, burst from the factor's lips in an irresistible flood.

'Aye, I shot Joe Bostock!' he cried. 'Often I'd warned him what would be if ever he came betwixt me and mine. And when he sent Will Carruthers there to steal Molly from me — for I ken weel that was Joe's doing — I knew the time had come.

'Tom Bowyer there had a hold on me. Aye, Tom, your time's come now, and I've listened to ye so long ye'll listen to me. He was ever at me — threatening me with the auld threat if I didna obey. 'Remember, Donald McDonald, so long as Joe lives, ye live only by sufferance of mine!' he would say to me. When he came to the store a year ago I spoke of Will Carruthers, and how I feared he'd been sent by Joe to take Molly away from me. 'Your chance will come, McDonald,' he said. 'Ye'll catch the twa o' them in the bush someday togither.' 'I ha' one death on my soul now,' I said. He laughed that fox-laugh of his. 'Ye're afraid,' he taunted me. And that taunt and laugh put the de'il into me.

' 'Listen, now, McDonald,' he said, 'if ye could kill Joe Bostock and no suspeecion come on ye, would ye do it?' He knew the rancor that was like a living coal in my heart, and he saw that he'd won. Then he told me his plan. I was to pretend a stroke, so that my foot would be useless, and my arm would hang useless at my side. Then, he said, there'd be no possible suspeecion on me. He brought me a book to read about it in. And, as he said, 'twas nought to feign a stroke — nought at all. Just to lie down and breathe heavy, and never forget I couldna use my arm or leg.

'He went awa' and left me wi' the thocht. It grew in me until it filled my heart. Then one nicht he cam' to me — Molly didna know that — and he told me that Joe and Will Carruthers were coming to the portage, and I could catch them alone. The chance came. Jules was in the bush, and Molly'd gone to the Indian camp.

'I slipped out o' bed and took the rifle

and one cartridge, put on my snowshoes, and ran across the muskeg. It wasna long before I saw them on the ridge, black against the gray sky. I crept up behind the rocks till I was a hundred paces awa'. Joe Bostock's back was turned. I drew a bead on his heart and fired. They baith fell down. I ran back to the store and went to bed. Jules didna see me, and Molly hadn't come hame.'

He groaned and hung his head upon his breast. The voice of Payne cut the silence like a knife.

'You are telling this of your free will, McDonald?' he asked.

'As God is my witness! I'm tellin' this because my time's come now, and I wouldna have Will Carruthers swing for that red fox yonder!'

'What was the nature of Mr. Bowyer's hold on you, McDonald?'

The crown attorney stood up with a wry smile. 'I object to that question,' he said quietly.

'I'll put it this way, then: Why did you hate Joe Bostock?'

'Aye, and I'll tell that, too,' answered

McDonald. 'Joe was married when he was a young man, long ago. A good girl. A sweet lass from my ane town in Scotland. They were both young. They quarreled. She wanted to vex him. She made up a story that showed her to be a bad woman. She went too far. Joe believed her. She went to him and told him that she'd lied. He wouldna believe her word. Because the foolish girl had manufactured proofs — false proofs; and the lying scoundrel whom she trusted claimed they were true.

'He blackmailed her after Joe had left her. She was at her wits' end. She went to his office to beg him to tell the truth. I happened to go there. I overheard. She became frenzied and drew a revolver on him. He struck her. He got her by the throat. He had a paperweight on the table, a sharp-edged metal thing like a cleaver. I struck him once with it. It split his skull from side to side. He died. E'en while I watched him, he died.

'The girl was mad wi' fear. I took her awa'. I married her, for Joe had divorced her in the States. But that fox, Bowyer, knew. In my folly I'd told him all. He said he'd be my friend. He got me my poseetion at the portage. I've lived there ever since — first with my wife, then with my fears, and always with Molly — with Molly, her child and — Joe's!'

The girl's cry rang wildly through the courtroom. She reeled and ran toward him. Wilton, unhindered, stooped down from the dock and supported her. She clung to him, wild-eyed and helpless. Nobody intervened.

Even when Bowyer sprang forward, though the judge rapped his gavel smartly, it seemed only an automatic or perfunctory act, for he made no effort to prevent his speaking.

'Let me finish it!' he yelled fiercely. 'He didn't die, you fool — you old fool; Lord, you've been a laughing-stock these twenty years! He's here in the court, and he's been blackmailing me as he blackmailed you. Clark, master-forger and safe-breaker — though we didn't need you for that — step forward! Look at his head! Look at the scar across his head, McDonald, and then see if you remember him!

'He's spoken true! The old fool's spoken true! I've handled many a man and woman in my time, but God himself, they say, can't handle a fool.' He swung round on his accomplices. 'Keep your wits, Phayre!' he howled in wild derision. 'You didn't know how Joe died. You're only the thief — the common thief I hired to work for me. You won't swing for this. Neither will I. I took my chances — but, by God, I couldn't handle a fool!'

They rushed toward him, but Bowyer was quicker than they. And, as the single shot echoed through the courtroom, Wilton saw that Molly was already mercifully unconscious.

But he knew that all the past would become dimmed with her awakening.

COLIN'S GHOST

Norman Firth

In the uncharted jungle of Peru, explorers Colin Davis and Arthur Birnes find the lost city of Kosan, overflowing with gold and gems. Davis intends to share their discovery with the world, but Birnes has more avaricious aims — and he's ready to murder for them . . . Waiting to meet with an informant, undercover policeman Danny King is instead approached by a young woman who claims she is in danger. And as he escorts her home, Danny is jumped by two thugs . . .

WRAITH OF VENGEANCE

Edmund Glasby

Contemplating a scheme to plunder a sinister Venetian island of a rumoured hoard, a tour company advisor finds more there than he bargained for . . . The group gathered for the reading of a will get the shock of their lives . . . A distant oil-drilling platform endures a bizarre siege . . . A man undergoes a hideous transformation . . . The night shift in a morgue takes a deadly turn . . . In an English village on All Hallows Eve, an ancient evil reawakens. Six tales of horror and the macabre by Edmund Glasby.

SILENCE OF THE BONES

Arlette Lees

Rodeo star Coby Dillon vanishes in a storm on the very evening he was to set up house with his girlfriend Brielle Broussard. Where is he — and what has become of his mentor Dyce Dean Jackson? Meanwhile, Deputy Sheriffs Robely Danner and Frack Tilsley — partners in both work and love — are investigating reports of poisonous contaminated moonshine. And Robely's mother Gladys Calhoun is brutally attacked in the night. All these seemingly disparate events are connected by a thread of blood . . .

THE TOKEN

Gerald Verner

Four murders in just over a month, and not the ghost of a clue as to who has committed them — except that in each case a little silver bell was left on the body of the victim. Under pressure from all quarters, Detective-Inspector Shadgold seeks the help of his friend Trevor Lowe, the famous criminologist. But Lowe has nothing to go on, either — until he is approached by terrified film star Gloria Swayne, who reveals that the first victim of the silver bell killer had been her secret fiancé . . .

MYSTERY OF THE RUBY

V. J. Banis

According to legend, the Baghdad ruby has the power to grant anything the heart desires. But a curse lies upon it, and all who own the stone are destined to die tragically, damned for eternity. When Joseph Hanson inherits the gem after his uncle's bizarre murder, his wife Liza is afraid. Though his fortune grows, he becomes surly and brutal. And suddenly Liza knows there's only one way to stave off the curse of centuries — she must sacrifice her own soul to save the man she loves.

LONELY BUSINESS

Steven Fox

Herbie Vore, mystery writer and recent widower, leads a lonely, uneventful existence — until he begins to receive threatening postcards and packages referring to Cindy, his crush from long ago. When a teenager arrives at his door claiming to be the son of his old flame, Herbie learns that Cindy has also been receiving mysterious notes and phone calls. Who could want to harm them after all these years — and why? The investigation will uncover more than Herbie ever imagined — and possibly cost him his life . . .